GONE FISHIN'

"Fans already needing a fix after Mosley's *A Little Yellow Dog,* get happy: Easy and Mouse are back in this prequel. . . . Mosley delivers the goods every time, and Easy fans are going to eat this up."

—*Library Journal*

"*Gone Fishin'* firmly establishes Mosley as a writer whose work transcends the thriller category and qualifies as serious literature. . . . Mosley displays a pitch-perfect gift for capturing the cadences of black speech that rivals the dialogue in Ralph Ellison's *Invisible Man.*"

—*Time*

"A powerfully raw, lyrical coming-of-age story. . . . This late encounter with the early Easy offers an extra dimension to readers who have met, in previous stories, the man he grew to be."

—*Publishers Weekly*

DEVIL IN A BLUE DRESS

"I read *Devil in a Blue Dress* in one sitting and didn't want it to end. An astonishing first novel."

—Jonathan Kellerman

"The social commentary is sly, the dialogue fabulous, the noir atmosphere so real you could touch it. A first novel? That's what they say. Amazing. Smashing."

—*Cosmopolitan*

"Richly atmospheric . . . *Devil in a Blue Dress* honors the hard-boiled tradition of Hammett/Chandler/Cain in its story line and attitude, but Mosley takes us down some mean streets that his spiritual predecessors never could have. . . . A fast-moving, entertaining story written with impressive style. This is the kind of book that leaves you yearning to read more about Easy Rawlins' adventures."

—*Los Angeles Times Book Review*

"A strong novel, with a skillful understanding of the genre and a lively talent for invention."

—*The New Yorker*

"A sparkling debut novel . . . [A] rich storytelling legacy is constantly and wonderfully present in *Devil in a Blue Dress*."

—*Chicago Tribune*

"A beautifully realized homage to hard-boiled fiction. . . . Mosley has given American crime fiction another unique hero and a solid mystery, all the way to the brilliant, existential last page."

—*San Francisco Chronicle*

"This guy has the magic. *Devil in a Blue Dress* is, without question, the most self-assured, uniquely voiced first novel I've ever read. Mosley's going to be compared with Chandler, but he has a clarity and precision that Chandler never achieved—and a relevance."

—Andrew Vachss

"Mosley has a lot of fun upending our preconceptions. . . . Best of all is Mosley's main creation, Easy Rawlins, a man as hard-nosed as he needs to be, yet still capable of relishing decency when he finds it."

—*Newsweek*

A LITTLE YELLOW DOG

"The best book yet in this fine series. Easy Rawlins [is] one of the most distinctive voices in crime fiction."

—Seattle Times

"[A] well-energized and crafty volume."

—The New York Times Book Review

BLACK BETTY

"Detective fiction at its best—bold, breathtaking, and brutal."

—Chicago Sun-Times

"As always, Mosley's grip on character is compelling."

—People

WHITE BUTTERFLY

"Rawlins . . . might be the best American character to appear in quite some time."

—Entertainment Weekly

"Compelling. . . . In all of American fiction, only Richard Wright treats America's race problem more savagely."

—Village Voice Literary Supplement

A RED DEATH

"Fascinating and vividly rendered . . . exotic and believable, filled with memorable and morally complex situations."

—The Wall Street Journal

"Exhilaratingly original."

—Philadelphia Inquirer

WALTER MOSLEY

GONE FISHIN'

AN EASY RAWLINS MYSTERY

WASHINGTON SQUARE PRESS
NEW YORK LONDON TORONTO SYDNEY SINGAPORE

This book is a work of fiction. Names, characters, places and incidents are products of the author's imagination or are used fictitiously. Any resemblance to actual events or locales or persons, living or dead, is entirely coincidental.

WSP

A Washington Square Press Publication of
POCKET BOOKS, a division of Simon & Schuster, Inc.
1230 Avenue of the Americas, New York, NY 10020

Copyright © 1997 by Walter Mosley
"Smoke" copyright © 2002 by Walter Mosley

Published by arrangement with Black Classic Press

All rights reserved, including the right to reproduce this book or portions thereof in any form whatsoever.
For information address Black Classic Press,
4701 Mount Hope Drive, Suite B, Baltimore, MD 21215

ISBN: 978-0-7434-5175-8

First Washington Square Press trade paperback printing September 2002

20 19 18 17

WASHINGTON SQUARE PRESS and colophon are registered trademarks of Simon & Schuster, Inc.

Cover art by Don Kilpatrick III

Printed in the U.S.A.

For information regarding special discounts for bulk purchases, please contact Simon & Schuster Special Sales at 1-800-456-6798 or business@simonandschuster.com

FOR MY MOTHER
ELLA
—WM

SMOKE

EASY," SHE SAID, and then the phone rang. Or maybe it was the other way around. Maybe the phone rang, and then Bonnie called my name.

Bright sun shone in the window, and the skies were clear as far as I could see. There was a beautiful woman of the Caribbean lying next to me. From the living room, early morning cartoons were squeaking softly while Feather giggled as quietly as she could. Somewhere below the blue skies, Jesus was hammering away, building a single mast sail that he intended to navigate toward some deep unknown dream.

It was one of the most perfect mornings of my life. I had a steady job, a nice house with a garden in the backyard, and a loving family.

But I was nowhere near happy.

The phone rang again.

"Easy," Bonnie said.

"I hear it."

"Daddy, phone," Feather yelled from her TV post.

Her dog, Frenchie, growled in anger just to hear her say something to me.

Jesus stopped his hammering.

The phone rang again.

"Honey," Bonnie insisted.

I almost said something sharp, but instead I grabbed the receiver off the night table.

"Yeah?"

"Ezekiel?"

Ezekiel is my given name but I never use it. So when that deep voice came out of the phone, I stalled a moment, wondering if it was asking for someone else.

"Ezekiel?" the voice said again.

"Who is this?"

"I'm lookin' for Raymond," the near-bass voice said.

"Mouse is dead."

I sat up, pulling the blankets from Bonnie's side of the bed. She didn't reach for the sheets to cover her naked body. I liked that. I might have even smiled.

"Oh no," the voice assured me. "He ain't dead."

"What?"

"No." The voice was almost an echo. There was a click and I knew that the connection had been broken.

"Easy?" Bonnie said.

I put the phone back into its cradle.

"Easy, who was it?"

Bonnie pressed her warm body against my back. The memory of Raymond's death brought about the slight nausea of guilt. Add that to the heat of the woman I loved and I had to pull away. I went to the window.

Down in the backyard I saw the frame of Jesus's small boat on orange crates and sawhorses in the middle of the lawn.

"It was . . . a woman I think. Deep voice."

"What did she want?"

"Mouse."

"Oh. She didn't know he was dead," Bonnie said in that way she had of making everything okay with just a few words.

"She said he was alive."

"What?"

"I don't think she *knew*. It was more like she was certain that he couldn't be dead."

"That's just the way people think about him," Bonnie said.

"No. It was something else."

"What do you mean?"

I went back to the bed and took Bonnie's hands in mine. "Do you have to leave today?" I asked her.

"Sorry."

Jesus's hammer started its monotonous beat again.

Feather turned up the volume on Crusader Rabbit now that she knew we were awake.

"I know you got to go," I said. "But . . ."

"What?"

"I dreamt about my father last night."

She reached out and touched my cheek with her palm. Bonnie had work-woman hands, not callused, but hard from a long life of doing for herself and others.

"What did he say?" she asked me.

That was her superstitious streak. She believed that the dead could speak through dreams.

"He didn't say a thing," I said. "Just sat there in a chair on a raft in the water. I called out to him four or five times before he looked up. But just then the current started pullin' the raft downstream. I think he saw me but before he could say anything he was too far away."

Bonnie took my head in her arms and held on tight. I didn't try to pull away.

WE SAT DOWN TO BREAKFAST at nine o'clock, two hours after I was supposed to be at work. Jesus had taken Feather to school. After that he was going to work four hours as a box boy at Tolucca Market on Robertson. In the late afternoon he'd come back home and read to me from *Treasure Island*. That was our deal: he'd read out loud to me for forty-five minutes and then discuss what he had read for three quarters of an hour more. He did that every day, and I agreed to let him drop out of high school.

Jesus wasn't interested in a public school education, and there was nothing I could do to light a fire under him. He was smart about things he cared for. He knew everything about grocery stores because of his job. He worked there and did gardening around our neighborhood to afford his boat dreams. He liked carpentry and running. He loved to cook and explore the beaches up and down the coast around L.A.

"What are you thinking about?" Bonnie asked.

We were holding hands under the table like schoolchildren going steady.

"Juice," I said. "He's doin' pretty good."

"Then why do you look so sad?"

"I don't know. Maybe it's that phone call."

Bonnie leaned closer and squeezed my hand. "I'm going to be gone longer than usual," she said.

"How long?"

"Maybe three or four weeks. Air France is having a special junket around western Africa with black political leaders and some European corporate heads. They need a French-speaking black stewardess who can also speak English. They'll need me on call for special flights."

"Oh. Yeah." It felt like she was punishing me for feeling bad.

"I told you that I'd have to be gone sometimes," she said sweetly.

"That's okay," I said. "Just don't go believin' it when one'a those men says that he wants to make you his queen."

HUNDREDS OF CHILDREN were assembled in front of Sojourner Truth Junior High School when I arrived—three and a half hours late.

"Mr. Rawlins," Archie "Ace" Muldoon said, greeting me on the granite stair of the main building. Short and balding, the little white man doffed his White Sox baseball cap in deference to his boss—me.

"Hey, Ace. What's happenin' here?"

"Fire in the metal shop bungalow."

"But that's down on the lower campus. Why they wanna evacuate up here?"

"Mr. Newgate." That's all he needed to say. Our principal, Hiram Newgate, was the source of all discord and wasted energy.

"Rawlins, I want to talk to you," Newgate said from the entrance hall. It was as if Archie conjured him up by saying his name.

"What about, Hiram?" I called back.

Newgate's lip curled into a snarl at my disrespectful tone.

He was tall and scarecrow-thin with cheekbones that were almost as high as his eyes. He would have been ugly if he didn't have perfect grooming, bright white and immaculate teeth, and clothes bought only in the finest Beverly Hills stores. That day he was wearing a shark-gray jacket and slender-cut black slacks.

He was looking good but I had outdone him. I was dressed in one of my best suits; off-white linen with felt buff shoes, brown argyle socks and tan shirt that I kept open at the collar due to the nature of my job, which was supervising senior head custodian.

I liked dressing up because of my background, which was poor and secondhand. But it also gave me a secret pleasure to see Newgate look me up and down, comparing my clothes to his.

"Where have you been?" the jade-eyed principal asked me.

I shrugged, not having enough respect for the man to lie.

"That's not an acceptable answer."

"What's the fire report, Archie?" I asked my custodian.

"Fire captain's down in the yard," the small man said.

"Mr. Rawlins," Principal Newgate sputtered. "I'm speaking to you."

"Sorry, Hiram," I said as I walked away. "But I'm late and there's going to be a lot of paperwork around this fire."

"What?" he exclaimed. He probably said a lot more, but I touched Archie's arm and we went quickly toward the stairway that led down to the lower campus.

❀   ❀   ❀

THE METAL SHOP bungalow was slightly scorched when the firemen arrived. They had reduced the building to splinters by the time they were through.

It was a strange vision for me. A burnt and shattered building surrounded by white men dressed in red. They were all young and grinning. Outside the nearby chain-link fence were dozens of men and women among the displaced students—all of them black or brown—staring wide-eyed at the demolition. I could feel my heart thumping and my hands getting hot.

A fireman approached us. He was hatless and haggard, no older than I, but he looked to be ready for retirement. He was making his way toward us with a deliberate and tired gait.

"You the principal?" the old-looking fireman asked. His gray pupils were watery, almost white.

"No," I said. "My name is Rawlins. I'm the plant supervisor."

"Where's the principal?"

"Mosta the kids're on the upper campus. He's makin' like a general on his horse up there, keepin' the troops from deserting."

That got a laugh from the fire captain. He reached out to shake my hand.

"Gregson," he said. "I'm the shift commander. Looks like you got a problem here."

I glanced at the poor colored people looking in at those uniformed marauders. I wondered if Gregson and I saw the same problems.

"It's arson," the fireman continued. "We found a scorched gasoline can under the building. It's a pretty sophisticated incendiary smoke bomb."

"They set it off with people in there?"

"Weren't you here?" Gregson asked me.

"I was late today."

"Oh. Well, somebody pulled the fire alarm and then set off the device, or maybe they set it off and then pulled the alarm. Maybe someone else saw the smoke but I doubt it; the people in the classroom hadn't even seen it yet. They pulled the alarm on the wall of the janitors' bungalow."

I BORROWED SOME LINED PAPER and a pencil from one of the students, through the fence, and took down all the information: Gregson's phone number, the police number to call to give information to the arson squad, and the names and numbers of the forms I had to fill out. He told me that an inspector would show up in the afternoon. All the while the firemen prowled around the shattered building, using their axes just in case some embers still burned.

I went up to Principal Newgate's office after that. I detested the man but he was still my boss.

"I'll buzz him, Mr. Rawlins," Kathy Langer said.

Everything about her was brown except for her skin: eyes, hair, dress, and shoes. She was a young white woman, a new transfer to Truth. Hiram's secretaries were always new, because they never lasted very long. He was always complaining about how they filed or typed. The last one left because he yelled at her for forgetting to put three sugar cubes into his coffee.

"It's Mr. Rawlins," she said into the phone. Then she looked up at me and said, "Just a minute. He's finishing a call." She smiled when she saw me looking at her drab clothes. It was the kind of smile that had gotten many young black men hung down South.

"Police?"

"No," she said as she inclined her head, showing me her throat. "Some guy who's been calling. I think it's personal business."

A moment later the buzzer sounded and she said, "You can go in now."

I hadn't been in Newgate's office for a few weeks and was surprised at the change in decor. I suppose the shock showed on my face.

"What?" Newgate said. He was sitting behind a beat-up ash-blond desk.

"What happened to all your fancy furniture?"

When Newgate became principal, he had brought expensive ebony wood and teak furniture with him. Along with the carpeting, his office had looked like a rich man's den. Now the floors were bare, the desk looked to be due for disposal, and his books and papers were in stacks along the walls.

"I bought a new house," he said. "I took the furniture for the living room."

"Why didn't you tell me? I coulda come up with a decent desk and some shelves." I knew the answer to my question before I finished asking it. He didn't want to ask me for anything. I was too uppity and confident for him to request my help. It's not that he had a problem with my color; Newgate wanted everybody to treat him like the master.

"What do you have on the fire?" he asked.

"Arson."

The principal paled visibly. "While the students were in

class? They could have been killed." He was talking to himself more than to me. "That's, that's horrible."

"I don't think anybody coulda been killed," I said. "Fire captain told me that even though they used a gasoline can it was pretty much just a smoke bomb."

"A kid's prank?"

"Naw. He said the bomb was very professional-looking."

Newgate and I stared at each other for a moment. "What do you think, Mr. Rawlins?"

What I thought was that Hiram Newgate had never asked me what I thought about anything. But what I said was, "I hope that it's just a one-time thing. Not some kind of craziness."

"What do you mean?"

"I wish I knew."

"Well," he said, still shaken. "I'm sure that it's just some kid with a problem. If he does something like this again we'll find him."

"I hope you're right."

"I have a doctor's appointment at noon so I'll be out midday. If the police come you give them what they need."

THE REST OF THE DAY was pretty noneventful. No more fires or fire alarms. No plumbing or electrical disasters. It was actually a good day because Newgate wasn't around looking into everybody's business. He bothered the teachers as much as he did the custodial staff. He often walked into classrooms unannounced to make surprise evaluations. That might have been a good idea, but Newgate was rude and rough. He loved Truth more than anyone, but not a soul there cared for him.

* * *

THAT AFTERNOON I was out inspecting the lower yard when First Wentworth called me. First was a small boy, thirteen at the time. Like many of the young children, he spent his summers hanging around the schoolyard, taking advantage of the facilities we offered for daycare. He played caroms and tetherball from ten, when the playground opened, until two, when it closed. After that I let him work with me, moving desks out of the classrooms so that my custodians could strip the floors and seal them for the new school year.

"Mr. Rawlins," he called from halfway down the eighty-seven stairs leading to the upper, older, campus. At least I think he said my name. I just heard his voice and saw him running down the granite steps.

While he ran I continued my inspection, looking into the trash cans on the yard. In one can I found a beaded white sweater that some child had discarded. It was a nice sweater, one hundred percent cotton. It represented a few days' labor out of a poor woman's pay, I knew. But clothes for children are like skin on snakes: to be shed now and then, allowing the new child to emerge.

"Mr. Rawlins," First said when he reached me.

I put the sweater under my arm. "Hey, Number One."

"I don't know what he was doin' over there." First was talking as if we were already in the middle of a conversation. "But I saw him."

"Who?"

"That white man."

"What white man?"

"The one who put that thing under Mr. Sutton's classroom."

"What thing?"

"A big red can," the boy said. "I don't know why."

"Why didn't you say anything before this?" I asked.

"I forgot that I saw'im. But then later Mr. Weston said that the school might burn down."

I could have asked him why he came to me, but I knew the answer. I was the only black person on the campus who had any authority. Most of the children came to me with their problems because bill collectors, policemen, and angry store owners were the only white people in their daily lives.

"And it was a white man?" I asked First.

He nodded, looking at my feet.

"Was he wearin' a suit?"

"Uh-uh. Just some pants and a green windbreaker."

"Have you seen him around here before?" I asked. "Does he work here sometimes?"

First shook his head. "No. I mean I seen'im but he don't work here."

"Where'd you see him?"

"Wit' Cousin."

"Who's that?"

"It's a boy, a man. You know."

"A young man?"

"Uh-huh, he used to go here. But he graduated an' dropped out." First looked up at me. "Am I in trouble?"

"No, Number One. You did all right. You might have to tell somebody else about it. But don't worry right now. Don't you have a class to go to?"

"Yeah. History-geography."

"You better go then."

I watched the child, who was so willing to rely on my strength, run up all those eighty-odd stairs without a falter.

I CALLED THE POLICE STATION and asked for Sergeant Andre Brown. When he wasn't there, I talked to another policeman; I forget his name. I forget because he was of no help. He told me to come in the next afternoon and file a report. When I said that I thought it might be more important than that, he hung up.

Then I called the fire department. Gregson was out on a call. When I told the operator why I was calling, he told me to call the police.

"ALL I KNOW IS that his nickname was Cousin," I said to Laini Trellmore, Sojourner Truth's registrar.

"Cousin. Hm," the elderly woman said to herself. She looked closer to seventy-five than the age she gave, which was sixty-one. I wasn't the only one to suspect that under her duties as record keeper, Miss Trellmore had altered her date of birth to keep her job past the age of forced retirement.

She frowned.

"Oh yes. I remember now. Douglas Hardy. Oh yes. Trouble from the first day to the last. He was sixteen years old and still in the ninth grade. Oooo. The kind of boy who's always grinning and nodding and you know he just did something bad."

"You got an address for his family in the files?"

THE HARDY FAMILY lived on Whithers Court off of Avalon. It was a dead-end street that had once been nice. Neat little

single-family homes built for working people in a cul-de-sac.
But the houses had all been bought up by a real estate syndi-
cate called Investors Group West. They raised the rent as
much as the market would bear. The turnover in tenants had a
harmful influence on the upkeep of the dwellings and the
street. Barren lawns and walls with the paint peeling off were
the norm.

The Hardys' home was secured by a screen door frame that
had no screen. There was loud cowboy music blaring from
inside. I looked for a doorbell but there was none. I knocked
on the door, but my knuckles were no match for the yodeling
cowboy.

I pulled the door open and took a tentative step inside. It
was that step, uninvited into the house of people who were
strangers to me, that was the first step outside the bounds of
the straight and narrow life that I pretended to. The room
had a gritty look to it. Dust on the blanket-covered sofa and
dust on the painted wood floor. The only decoration was a
paper calendar hung by a nail on the far wall. It had a large
picture of Jesus, his bleeding Valentine's heart protruding
from his chest, over a small booklet of months. There was no
sign of life.

I considered calling out, but I would have had to shout to
be heard over the warbling cowboy, and anything that loud
might alarm any occupants of that tinderbox home.

I turned off the radio.

"What the hell is goin' on?" someone said from beyond a
doorway that led to the kitchen.

A short brown woman hustled in. She was wearing a shape-
less blue shift that had white butterflies all over it. The neck of

the dress had been stretched out, one side sagging open over her left shoulder.

"Who the hell are you?" she asked, squinting and scowling so that I could see the red gums of her almost toothless maw.

"Ezekiel," I said, remembering the morning caller.

"What the hell do you want?"

"I'm lookin' for Cousin."

Her nose twitched as if she were tied to a post and a mosquito were trying to bite her nose.

"Rinaldo!"

I heard a man grunt somewhere in the house. The heavy pounding of footsteps followed and soon a man, not as short as the woman but not as tall as I, came through the doorway. He was wearing only boxer shorts and a yellow T-shirt. His nose, chin, and forehead jutted out from the face as if his head were meant to be used as an axe. His eyes seemed insane, but I put that down to him getting rousted by the woman's scream.

"What, Momma?"

"This man lookin' for Cousin."

"The hell are you?" Rinaldo asked me.

"Cousin's in trouble," I said.

"The fuck he is," Rinaldo said.

"Watch your language, boy," Toothless Mama said.

"The hell are you?" Rinaldo asked again. He balled his fists and levered his shoulders to show off a ripple of strength.

"He knows a man who tried to burn down the junior high school," I said. "Somebody saw them together—"

"Who?" the woman asked.

Ignoring her, I kept on talking to Hatchet Face. ". . . if I don't see me some Cousin I'm just gonna give the police this address and let you shake your shoulders at them."

Rinaldo's eyes got crazier as he woke up. He seemed torn between attack and flight. He was fifteen years my junior, but I felt that I could take him. It was Mama who scared me. She was the kind of woman who kept a straight razor close at hand.

"Cousin didn't start that fire," Mama said.

"How would you know?"

"He was here with us."

"Where is he now?"

Mama and Rinaldo exchanged glances. They were afraid of the police. They had good reason to be. All black people had good reason to be. But I didn't care.

"Tell me or I'll go right down to the precinct," I said.

"He live on Hooper," Rinaldo said. He blurted out an address.

"Okay," I said, and I took a step backward. "I'ma go over there. If somebody calls him and warns him off I'm sendin' the cops here to you."

Rinaldo gave his mother a sharp look. Maybe he wondered if he should try to kill me. I took another step back. Before they could decide on an action, I was out of the door and on the way to my car. Rinaldo came out to watch me drive off.

"WHO IS IT?" a voice asked after I knocked.

"Are you Cousin?" I asked.

There was a pause, and then, "Yeah?"

"I'm John Lowry. Rinaldo sent me."

When he opened the door, I punched him in the face. It was a good solid punch. It felt good but it was a stupid thing to do. I didn't know who else was in the room. That crouching, slack-jawed man might have been a middleweight contender. He could have had an iron jaw and a pistol in his pocket. But I hit him because I knew that he had something to do with the fire at my school, because Mama and Rinaldo set my teeth on edge, because the police didn't seem to care what I did, and because my best friend was dead.

Cousin fell flat on his back.

The room was painted a garish pink and there was no furniture except for a single mattress no thicker than a country quilt.

"Get up," I said.

"What I do to you, mister?" he whined.

"Why you try'n burn down the school?"

"I didn't burn nuthin'." Cousin got to his feet.

He was an old twenty. Not smart or mature, just old. Like he had lived forty years in half the time but hadn't learned a thing.

I knocked him down again.

"Hey, man!" he yelled.

"Who's the white man you were with?"

"What white man?"

"You want me to kick you?" I moved my right foot backward in a threatening motion.

"What you want from me?"

"The man put that bomb under the metal shop at Truth."

Cousin's skin was a deep, lusterless brown. His jaw was swelling up. He passed his hand over his head from fear that I'd mussed his hair.

"You the law?"

"I work for the school."

"Man named Lund."

"Lund?"

"Uh-huh."

"How you spell it?"

"I'on't know, man."

"What do you know?" I asked in disgust.

"Roke Williams. Roke run a crap game down Alameda. Lund work for the man sell him p'otection."

I DROVE TO A SMALL BUILDING on Pico and Rimpau. All the way I was wondering why a man in organized crime would be setting a bomb at a Negro junior high school. I wondered but I wasn't afraid—and that was a problem. If you go up against men in organized crime, you should at least have the sense to be afraid.

There was a weathered sign above the front door of the building. If you looked closely you could make out the word HETTLEMANN and, a little farther down, RINGS. I had no idea what the building used to be. Now it was a series of sales and service offices rented out to various firms and individuals. On the fourth floor was a block of offices run by a man named Zane. They did bookkeeping and financial statements for small businesses.

The three flights of stairs was nothing for me. For the past few months I had cut down to ten cigarettes a day and I was used to the vast stairway at Truth.

When I opened the door on the fourth floor, I came into a small room where Anatole Zane sat. Zane, by his own estimation was a ". . . manager, receptionist, janitor, and delivery

boy . . ." for his quirky accounting firm. He hired nonprofes-
sionals who were good with numbers and parceled out tasks
that he took in for cut-rate prices.

Jackson Blue was his most prized employee.

"Mr. Rawlins." Zane smiled at me. He got his large body
out of the chair and shook my hand. "It's so good to see you
again."

Zane did my year-end taxes. I owned three apartment
buildings around Watts and had the sense to know that a professional would do a better job with the government than I
ever could. I had introduced the modest bookkeeper to the
cowardly, brilliant, and untrustworthy Jackson Blue.

"Good to see you too, Anatole."

"Jackson's in his office doing a spreadsheet on the
Morgans."

"Thanks."

I went through the door behind Zane's small desk. There I
entered a hall so narrow that I imagined the fat manager
might get stuck trying to make it from one end to the other.

I knocked on the third door down.

"Yeah?"

"Police!"

I heard the screech of a chair on the floor and three quick
steps across the room. Then there was a moment of silence.

After that, a quavering voice: "Easy?"

A door down the hall opened up. A bespectacled Asian
man stuck his head out. When I turned in his direction, he
jumped back and slammed the door.

"Come on, Jackson," I said loudly. "Open up."

The door I had knocked on opened.

If coyotes were black, Jackson Blue would have been their king. He was small and quick. His eyes saw more than most, and his mind was the finest I had ever encountered. But for all that, Jackson was as much a fool as Douglas "Cousin" Hardy. He was a sneak thief, an unredeemable liar, and dumb as a post when it came to discerning motivations of the human heart.

"What the fuck you mean scarin' me like that, Easy?"

"You at work, Jackson," I said, walking into his office. "This ain't no bookie operation. You not gonna get busted."

Jackson slammed his door.

"Shut up, man. Don't be talkin' like that where they might hear you."

I sat in a red leather chair that was left over from the previous tenants. Jackson had nice furniture and a fairly large office. He had a window too, but the only view was a partially plastered brick wall.

"How you doin', Jackson?"

"Fine. Till you showed up."

He crossed the room, giving me a wide berth, and settled in the chair behind his secondhand mahogany desk. He avoided physical closeness because he didn't know why I was there. Jackson had betrayed and cheated so many people that he was always on guard against attack.

"What you doin'?" I asked.

He held up what looked like a hand-typed manual. It had a cheap blue cover with IBM and BAL scrawled in red across the bottom.

Jackson smiled.

"What is it?"

"The key code to the binary language of machines."

"Say what?"

"Computers, Easy. The wave of the future right here in my hand."

"You gonna boost 'em or what?"

"You got a wallet in your pocket, right, man?"

"Yeah."

"You got some money in there?"

"What you gettin' at?"

"You might even have a Bank Americard, am I right?"

"Yes."

"One day all your money gonna be in this language here." He waved the manual again. "One day I'ma push a button and all the millionaires' chips gonna fall inta my wagon."

Jackson grinned from ear to ear. I wanted to slap him, but it wouldn't have made a difference. Here he was the smartest man you could imagine, and all he could think about was theft.

"Roke Williams," I said.

"Niggah was born in the alley and he gonna die in one too. Right down there offa Alameda."

"Who runs him?"

"Was a dude named Pirelli, but he got circulatory problems."

"Heart attack?"

"Kinda like. A bullet through the heart. Now it's a man named Haas. He's a slick bita business run his people outta the Exchequer on Melrose."

"How about a man named Lund?"

Jackson squinted and brought his long thumbs together. "No. Don't know no Lund. What's this all about, Easy?"

I told Jackson about the smoke bomb and Cousin.

When I finished he said, "So? What do you care about all that, man? It ain't your house."

"It's my job."

"Your job is to make sure that the toilets don't smell and that the trash cans is emptied. You not no bomb squad."

I remember trying to dismiss Jackson's argument as some kind of cowardly advice, but even then there was a grain of truth that made it through.

"Maybe not," I said. "But I'm in it now."

"You better bring some backup you wanna tango with Haas."

That reminded me of Mouse. He had been my backup since I was a teenager in Fifth Ward, Houston, Texas. Mouse was crazy, but he was always on my side.

"I got a call this mornin', Jackson. It was a woman with a deep bass voice—"

"She ask you about Mouse?"

"How you know that?"

"She called me too. Three days ago. Said she was lookin' for Raymond."

"What you say?"

Jackson became wary again. He scratched the back of his neck with his left hand and looked off to his left. When he saw that there was no escape route, he turned back to me. "I don't want no trouble now, Easy."

"Trouble's over, man. Mouse is dead."

"Like you once told me: you don't know that."

"I saw him. He wasn't breathin' and his eyes were wide. That bullet opened him up like a busted piñata."

"But you didn't go to no funeral."

"Etta carried the body outta the hospital. You know how much she loved him. She probably put him in the ground herself."

Jackson wrung his hands.

"What did you tell that woman?" I asked.

"Nuthin'. I didn't tell her a thing."

"Okay," I said. "What didn't you say?"

"You cain't tell nobody I told, Easy."

"Fine."

"A girl named Etheline, Etheline Teaman."

"What about her?"

"I met her a few weeks back and we started talkin' shit. I told her 'bout some'a the crazy stuff Mouse done did. You know, just talkin' jive. She told me that just before she left Richmond she met a gray-eyed, light-skinned brother named Ray. She said he got in a fight one night, and even though he was small, he put down this big dude with a chair, a bottle, and his knee. She didn't even know Mouse, man. She only moved here from Richmond six months ago."

"Where is this girl?"

"Piney's."

"A prostitute?"

"So what? You ain't askin' her to take care'a your kids. She said that she knew a man might be him. That's what you asked me."

"Why didn't you call me about this, Jackson?"

"If Mouse is alive and don't want nobody to know, then I don't need to say a word."

It was Jackson's long silence that bothered me. He turned

into a loudmouth braggart after just one beer. For him to have kept quiet about his suspicions meant that something in what he heard made him fear that Mouse was really alive.

And Mouse was a man to fear. He was deadly to begin with, and his heart was unrestrained by any feelings of guilt or morality.

"What you gonna do, Easy?"

"Go out and buy me a tie."

I STOPPED AT THE May Company downtown and bought an orange silk tie. It had blue veins running through it and a yellow kite veering to the side as if it had broken its string.

I knotted my tie using the rearview mirror and then drove off to Melrose Avenue.

The Exchequer hotel and bar was a small building wedged between a lamp store and a hospital for the elderly. Lined out on the sidewalk were the aged inmates of that old folks' prison. They sat in wheelchairs and on benches, looking out over Melrose as if it were the river Styx. I turned my head now and again as I passed them, thinking that one day, if I made it through this life, I would end up like them: discarded and broken at the side of the road.

There was one child-sized woman wearing a thin blue robe over blue pajamas. Her sagging, colorless eyes caught mine.

"Mister," she mouthed. Then she waved.

"Yeah, honey?" I crouched down in front of her.

"When you were a boy you were so beautiful," she whispered.

I smiled, wondering if my boyhood was showing in my face.

"Just like your mother," she said.

"You knew my mother?" I asked. Maybe she thought some black maid in the old days was my relation.

"Oh yes," she said, her voice getting stronger. "You're my grandson—Lymon."

Her eyes, when I first saw them, were beyond despair, verging on that stare that a dying man has when all hope of life is gone. I had seen many men during the war, shot up and dying, whose eyes had given up hope. But now the old lady's eyes overflowed with delight—her white grandson, me, filling their field of vision.

She reached out a hand and I took it. She leaned forward and I accepted the kiss on my cheek. I kissed her gray head and stood up.

"I'll come back a little later, Granny," I said. Then I walked off to meet with a gangster.

THE HOTEL LOBBY WAS SMALL and simple. Not elegant or tawdry, but plain. The registration desk could have been a bell captain's station. The rug would have to be changed in a year or less. The only outstanding features were the light fixtures set high up on the walls. They were in the form of nude women finished in shiny gold leaf. Above their heads they held big white globes of light.

"Help you?" the small man behind the desk asked. He was white and bald, about my age—which was mid-forties at the time. His eyes, nose, mouth, and ears were all too small for his small head. His miniature features showed disapproval and distrust of my presence. I couldn't blame him. How often did white people see black men in fancy suits in 1964?

"Lookin' for Mr. Haas," I said.

"Who are you?"

"You don't need to know my name, man."

The desk clerk ran his tongue up under his lower lip and looked over at a doorless doorway. He nodded toward the dark maw and I went.

"WHAT'S UP, ROCHESTER?" a white man with big ears asked me. He was standing at the bar.

"Could be your ticket," I said.

While he considered my words, I took a step closer to get within arm's distance, so that if he decided to go for a weapon, I could stop him before he stopped me.

"Fuck you," he said.

"Now that's better," I replied. "Are you Mr. Haas?"

"Who wants to know?"

"Ray," I said. "Ray Alexander. I need to talk some business with the man."

"Wait here."

Big Ears wore an ugly, copper-colored iridescent suit. As he shimmered away from me into the gloom of the bar, I wondered if I had gone crazy somehow without warning. Jackson Blue was right; I was way out of my prescribed world there at the Exchequer.

I had fallen back into bad habits.

"Can I help you?"

It was yet another white man, this time a bartender. His words offered help, but his tone was asking me to leave.

"Mr. Haas," I said, pointing toward the gloom.

A shimmering copper mass was emerging. Big Ears came up to me. "Come on."

*   *   *

IT WAS POSSIBLY the darkest room I had ever been in that wasn't intended for sleep. A man sat at a table under an intolerably weak red light. His suit was dark and his hair was perfect. Even though he was seated, I could tell that he was a small man. The only thing remarkable about his face were the eyebrows; they were thick and combed.

"Alexander?" he said.

I took a seat across from him without being bidden. "Mr. Alexander," I said.

His lips protruded a quarter inch; maybe he smiled. "I've heard of you," he ventured.

"I got a proposition. You wanna hear it?"

Ghostly hands rose from the table, giving his assent.

"There's a group of wealthy colored businessmen, from pimps to real estate agents, who wanna start a regular poker game. It's gonna float down around South L.A., some places I got lined up."

"So? Am I invited to play?"

"Five thousand dollars against thirty percent of the house."

Haas grinned. He had tiny teeth.

"You want I should just turn it over right now? Maybe you want me to lie down on the floor and let you walk on me too."

Haas's voice had become like steel. I would have been afraid, but because I was using Mouse's name, there was no fear in me.

"I'd be happy to walk on you if you let me, but I figure you got the sense to check me out first."

The grin fled. It was replaced by a twitch in the gangster's left eye.

"I don't do penny-ante shit, Mr. Alexander. You want to have a card game it's nothin' to me." He adjusted his shoulders like James Cagney in *Public Enemy*.

"Okay," I said. I stood up.

"But I know a guy."

I said nothing.

"Emile Lund," Haas continued. "He eats breakfast in Tito's Diner on Temple. He likes the cards. But he doesn't throw money around."

"Neither do I," I said, or maybe it was Raymond who said it and I was just his mouthpiece in that dark dark room way outside the limit of the law.

The old folks were gone when I emerged from the hotel. I missed seeing the old lady. I remember thinking that that old woman would probably be dead before I thought of her again.

FEATHER WAS ASLEEP in front of a plate with a half-eaten hot dog and a pile of baked beans on it. *Astro Boy*, her favorite cartoon, was playing on the TV. Jesus was in the backyard, hammering sporadically. I picked up my adopted daughter and kissed her. She smiled with her eyes still closed and said, "Daddy."

"How you know who it is?" I asked playfully. "You too lazy to open your eyes."

"I know your smell," she said.

"You have hot dogs?"

"Uh-huh."

"What you do at school all day?"

At first she denied that anything had happened or been learned at Carthay Circle elementary school. But after a while she woke up and remembered a bird that flew in her class-room window and how Trisha Berkshaw said that her father could lift a hundred pounds up over his head.

"Nobody better tickle him when he's doin' that," I said, and we both laughed.

Feather told me what her homework assignment was, and I set her up at the dinette table to get to work on her studies. Then I went outside to see Jesus.

He was rubbing oil into the timbers of his sailboat's frame.

"How's it goin', Popeye?" I asked.

"Sinbad," he said.

"Why you finishin' it before it's finished?"

"To make it waterproof inside and out," he said. "That's what the book says to do. That way if water gets inside it won't rot."

His face was the color of a medium tea; his features were closer to the Mayans than to me. He had deeper roots than the American Constitution in our soil. Neither of my children were of my blood, but that didn't make me love them less. Jesus was a mute victim of sex abuse when I found him. Feather's own grandfather had killed her mother in a parking lot.

"I got a lot to do the next few days, son," I said. "Could you keep close to home for Feather?"

"Can I have a friend come over?"

"Who?"

"Cindy Needham."

"Your girlfriend?"

Jesus turned his attention back to the frame. He could still be a mute when he wanted to be.

*   *   *

I MIGHT HAVE CLOSED my eyes sometime during the night, but I certainly didn't fall asleep. I kept seeing Raymond in that alley, again and again, being shot down while saving my life. At just about the same time John F. Kennedy was assassinated, but I never mourned our slain president. The last time I saw Mouse, his lifeless body was being taken to the hospital with a blanket covering his wounds.

TITO'S WAS A RECTANGULAR BUILDING raised high on cinder blocks. The inside had one long counter with two tables at the far end. Only one of the tables had an occupant. I would have bet the .38-caliber pistol in my pocket that that man was Emile Lund.

More than anything he looked like an evolved fish. There were wrinkles that went across his forehead and down along his balding temples. His eyes bulged slightly and his small mouth had pouting, sensual lips. His chin was almost nonexistent, and his hands were big. His shoulders were massive, so even though he looked like a cartoon, I doubted if anyone treated him that way.

The fish-man had been making notes in a small journal, but when I opened the door he looked up. He kept his eyes on me until I was standing at his table.

"Lund?" I asked. "I'm Alexander."

"Do I know you?"

"You wanna talk business or you wanna talk shit?" I said.

He laughed and held his big fins out in a gesture of apology.

"Come on, man. Don't be so sensitive. Sit down," Lund

said. "I know your rep. You're a man who makes money. And it's money makes my car go.

"Mona," Lund said to the woman behind the counter.

She was wearing a tight black dress that probably looked good on her twenty years before. Now it was just silly, like her brittle blond-dyed hair, her deep red lipstick, and all the putty pressed into the lines of her face and neck.

She waited for a bit, just to show that she didn't jump the minute someone called her name, and then walked over to our table. "Yeah?" the waitress said.

"What's your pleasure, Mr. Alexander?" Lund inquired.

"Scrambled eggs with raw onions on 'em, and a bottle of Tabasco sauce on the side." It was Mouse's favorite breakfast.

The waitress went away to pass my order on to the cook. Lund made a final note in his small journal, and then put the book away in a breast pocket.

"So, Mr. Alexander," he said. "You wanna play cards."

"I'm gonna play cards," I assured him. "I need a little seed money and some insurance against Roke Williams and the cops."

"From what I hear about you, you never buy insurance," the fish said.

"Man gets older he gets a little more conservative, smarter—you know."

The fish smiled at me, tending more toward shark than sardine. I took it in stride. After all, I wasn't the moderate custodian/landlord Easy Rawlins, I was the crazy killer Raymond Alexander. I was dangerous. I was bad. Nobody and nothing scared me.

The waitress came over with my eggs. I doused them with the hot sauce and shoveled them down.

"When do I get to see your game?" Lund asked me.

"Tonight if you want."

"Where?"

"We got a garage over on Florence." I took a slip of paper from my pocket and put it on the table. "That's the address."

"What time?"

"Nine-thirty would be too early. But anytime after that." My eggs were gone. I never liked raw onions and eggs before but I loved them right then. "You could sit in if you wanted to."

"Maybe so," he said. "Maybe so."

I WENT FROM TITO'S to the 77th Precinct.

Sergeant Andre Brown was in his small office. He was the highest-ranking black policeman in the station. And we had developed a sort of friendship.

Earlier that year there had been a gang killing of a student from Truth, and rumblings about bad blood between the gangs. I was able to point Brown in the direction of some bad eggs, making it possible for him to break up the trouble before it flared into a war.

Brown was in his thirties, tall and thin, with a thick mustache and a surprising deep laugh. He was a very clean man. Perfect nails and skin. His office had every book in place and every file in order. His graduation ring was from UCLA.

"Mr. Rawlins," he greeted me.

"Sergeant," I said. "How are you?"

"Fine. Just fine. I hear you had some problems at the school."

"Yeah." I sat down and stretched out my legs across his small office. "Yeah. That's kinda why I'm here."

Brown stood up and closed his door. This was something he'd never done before.

"Before you say anything," he said, "I have something to discuss with you."

"Okay. Shoot."

"The captain took me aside a few weeks ago and we had a talk about you."

"Yeah?"

"He told me to watch out for you. He said that you've been involved in some criminal activity and that you have been known to keep company with a hard-core criminal element." He looked at me, indicating that it was my turn to speak.

"I don't know what he said, but I'm no criminal, and I haven't been involved in any crimes," I said. That wasn't completely true, but it was close enough for Brown and I knew it. "It's true that I've known some pretty bad men, women too. If you go out your door down here you're likely to meet some bad folks, cain't help that. But what your captain might have meant is that I used to be in the business of doing favors."

"What kind of favors?"

"People, black people, got all kinds of difficulties, you know that. A kid gets mixed up with the wrong crowd, a car goes missing. Calling the police, many times, just makes something bad that much worse. In that kinda situation I would come in and give a little push. Nothing criminal. Nothing bad."

"Like an unlicensed private detective."

"Exactly like that. But you know I've been outta that business since coming to work at Truth."

Brown smoothed out one side of his mustache with a long

slender finger while he peered into my eyes. "Okay," he said at last. "All right. What can I do for you?"

That was my first experience with the second half of the twentieth century; the first time a man, black or white, holding a professional office, had given me the benefit of the doubt. He wasn't running a scam. He wasn't trying to get back at the police department. He simply saw my value and believed in my character.

"Have the kids in the gangs been messin' 'round wit' numbers or some other kinda gamblin'?" I asked.

"Not that I know of. I'm pretty sure not. Last group of kids I busted didn't have five dollars between them. Why?"

"I might know who set that smoke bomb at Truth."

"Who?"

"I won't be sure till tomorrow morning," I said. "The minute I know I'll turn it over to you."

Andre leaned forward in his chair. He was considering pushing me but decided against it. "Okay," he said.

We shook hands as equals, and I went off feeling like a new man. I was walking tall and flush with pride. But in spite of all that I wasn't even certain of my own name.

I WENT HOME to make sure that Feather and Jesus were okay, and then I made it back down to Florence. Bernard's Automotive Repair was managed by my oldest L.A. friend, Primo. He lived in the first house I ever owned. I still owned the house, and Primo never paid me a dime, so it was easy to get his keys to the garage for the night.

I unlocked the side door and turned on the radio in the mechanics' office. I switched on the office light and left the rest of the garage in darkness. Then I set myself up in a corner to the left of the door. Between my knees I had a baseball bat. On my lap was the .38. That was eight-fifteen.

IN THE DARK I HAD TIME to ponder my situation. There I was, waiting for more trouble than most citizens ever know. I had taken on Mouse's name and I was acting like him. It felt good, way too good. I expected Emile Lund to come in that door and see the light and hear the music. He'd be with one or two henchmen, but I had the element of surprise. I was a fool, I knew I was a fool, and still I didn't care.

Raymond Alexander had been the largest part of my history. My parents were both gone before I was nine. My relatives treated me like a beast of burden, so I ran from them. I fought a war for men who called me nigger. The police stopped me on the street for the crime of walking. Raymond was the only one who respected me and cared for me and was willing to throw his lot in with mine, no matter the odds.

I was sitting in that drafty corner because I didn't want Mouse to be dead. Somehow by using his name I felt that I was making a tribute, even a eulogy, to his meaning in my life.

THE IRIDESCENT GREEN HANDS on my watch said 11:03 when the door cracked open. Lund walked in alone. That worried me. If he'd come with a friend, it would have meant that he was cautious. A cautious man is more likely to be reasonable when facing a baseball bat and a pistol.

Lund was wearing jeans and a windbreaker, further proof that he was the man who bombed my classroom. I let him take two steps before pressing the gun barrel against the back of his neck.

"Hold it right there, man," I said in a husky, threatening tone.

Lund grunted and spun around, pushing my gun hand to the side. While he was concentrated on trying to disarm me, I hit him in the head with the bat. It was glancing blow and merely slowed him down. I hit him on the nose with the butt of my pistol, and he slowed a bit more. Fear was working its way into my gut because I realized that even though I was using Raymond's name, I'd never be able to inflict the kind of pain that he dished out. I pushed the angry gangster and he fell hard.

"Hold still, fool," I said.

But he ignored me and reached under the windbreaker. He was disoriented, so it was easy for me to kick the pistol out of his hand. He tried to crawl toward the gun, so I kicked him in the ribs. By this time I was getting sick. Nothing seemed to stop Lund. He struggled up to his knees and spat as if that would hold me off long enough for him to get his bearings. Blood was cascading from his nostrils, a high wheeze coming from his throat.

"Stop!" I yelled, but he got up on one foot.

I realized that I could either kill this man or run from him, but that I'd never subdue his spirit. He reminded me of a welterweight I'd seen, Carmen Basilio. That man would take punishment for twelve rounds or more, but he'd always come back, and in the last minutes he'd always win because his opponent was exhausted from waling away at the Italian boxer.

I unleashed a right uppercut that lifted Lund to his feet. Then I hit him with a straight left hand. Mouse would have hit him with the bat, repeatedly. I knew then that I would have to honor my friend in some other way.

Lund was unconscious, or nearly so. His eyes were half open and he was muttering something. I searched him and came up with his black book. I didn't think that it would help me much, but it was all I could get from him.

As I was going out of the door, Lund had gained his feet. He was still wobbly, searching the floor for his gun. I hurried out to the street.

DRIVING UP CENTRAL, I pondered my foolish actions. I thought that I'd just flash a gun at the gangster and he'd give me anything I wanted. I forgot about the dark alleys I'd once traveled. Hard men didn't get that way by turning over. Lund would have died before he bowed down to me.

I SAT UP IN MY LIVING ROOM, flipping through the pages of Lund's journal. There were multiple entries on every page. Each entry consisted of a name and a two- or three-letter code. At the bottom of each entry there was a date and a dollar amount. Roke Williams had several entries. He was paying Lund at least fifteen hundred dollars a month. Roke must have been making three times that amount. I knew that the gambler lived in a one-room apartment with the toilet down the hall. He made more in a month than most workingmen made in a year, and still he lived like a hermit crab.

One man, Vren Lassiter, had a special notation. In parentheses under his name were the initials "SchP." Lassiter had a minus sign next to his dollar amount. He owed over six thousand dollars.

It wasn't until I was undressed and in the bed, under the covers and almost asleep, that the initials made sense to me.

That was three A.M.

THE DRIVE FROM MY HOUSE near Fairfax and Pico down to Truth was only twenty-five minutes at three in the morning. Before four I was in the registrar's office looking up the faculty records.

HE WAS LIVING in an apartment building on San Pedro. It was a turquoise and plaster affair, designed to be ugly so that the tenants would know that they were poor.

I knocked on the door of apartment 3G. No one answered. I jiggled the knob and it turned.

He had lied about the furniture. He didn't use it for the new place. His big ebony desk wouldn't have fit through the front door. Hiram Newgate sold everything to pay Vren Lassiter's debt and now he was dead, slumped over on the thin cushions of a cheap couch, a .22-caliber bullet in his left temple, the pistol still in his hand.

I looked around the house. Photographs were spread across the card table in a nook that was supposed to be a dinette. The pictures were of two men, Hiram and a younger, sandy-headed man. They were arm-in-arm, holding hands. In one picture Hiram was laughing out loud.

I searched around for some kind of note, but there was none. I did find a letter though. It was from Lassiter. In it Vren beseeched his good friend to understand that he couldn't help making bets. He tried to kick the habit but he couldn't. And if Hiram didn't help, they'd probably kill him.

I figured that Newgate went to Lund and took on the debt, that Lund threatened the school because he figured out that Truth was more important to Hiram than his own life. Newgate had earned his own private abbreviation: SchP, School Principal.

I put the letter back into the desk and went to the front door. I turned to look one last time, to make sure that there was nothing I left behind. His eyes glittered as if they had moved. I came up to him and stared into those orbs. He was still alive. Paralyzed, but still alive. He saw me, knew me.

"It's gonna be all right, Principal Newgate," I said. I touched his cheek and nodded.

I made the anonymous call to the police from his phone and left. I was out of the neighborhood before the sirens came.

I WAITED TWO WEEKS before going to the 77th Precinct.

"Where'd you get this?" Andre Brown asked me at Leah's Doughnut and Coffee Shop three blocks down from the precinct. In his hand he held Emile Lund's notebook.

"Found it."

"If you found it, how would you know who it belongs to? His name's not in it anywhere."

"I guessed. I'm a good guesser, Officer."

"These are his clients?" Brown asked. He was becoming wary of me.

"Yeah. I guess."

Officer Brown studied me. He was a good study. Nine

times out of eleven he would come up with the solution to his inquiry—but not that morning.

"I hear they brought your principal back home yesterday," he said. "Some friend of his took him in?"

"Guy named Vren."

"That's an awful thing. Shoot yourself in the head and end up paralyzed for life."

I took a deep breath.

"What does this book have to do with the fire?" Andre asked.

"He's the one set the smoke bomb."

"How do you know that?"

"Read the book."

THAT NIGHT Feather sang us a song she'd learned in school. It was about a sailor lost at sea. He fought sea serpents and snake people and terrible storms. But at the end of the journey, he found a sunny land. And to his surprise, that sunny shore was the home he'd left long long ago.

"I learned it for Juice, Daddy," she said. "'Cause'a when he's in that boat he can sing it and then he could find his way back here."

"Me too, baby," I said. "Me too."

READ SIX EASY PIECES FOR THE CONCLUSION.

GONE FISHIN'

1

MOUSE HAD CHANGED.

Before he announced his engagement to EttaMae he was a happy man, full of himself. It's true that he was especially pleased when misfortune happened to someone else, but at least he kept us smiling. Life was hard back then and a good laugh was worth a month of Sundays.

But just when he had a reason to be glad, Mouse turned sour and moody. He let his appearance go to seed (he was usually a natty dresser) and nobody wanted to be around him because when a small, rodent-faced man like Mouse got ugly, he was no company even for the harshest man.

He stopped going to parties altogether. If you happened to run into him on some corner, or back alley, and asked how he was doing, he'd say, "What the hell you think? Here I am gonna get married in two months an' 'tween me an' EttaMae we ain't got enough money for dip an' crackers."

Mouse didn't go out looking for work. All he did was get mad whenever he had to let go of a few coins.

So it was no surprise that his crowd started to shun him.

I mean, even if you wanted to see Mouse it was hard work because he changed apartments almost every month—one step ahead of the landlord, as we used to say.

I didn't want to see him. Mostly because I was jealous. You see, EttaMae was the kind of woman you had on your mind when you woke up in the morning. She was big and friendly, and always knew the right thing to say. But she never lied; Etta spoke her mind, and when she laughed it came from her heart. Everybody loved EttaMae, and she loved the only man I ever knew who didn't have a heart at all.

SO BETWEEN ME being jealous and Mouse being so taciturn, I was surprised late one Tuesday night when a racket broke out at my apartment door. It sounded more like a fight than a knock. I dragged myself out of a deep sleep trying to think of who might be after me. I knew that it couldn't be the police, they just broke the door down in that neighborhood, and I hadn't seen any seriously married women in more than six months.

"Hold on!" I yelled, thinking about the back window. I was reaching for the butcher's knife on the nightstand when he called, "Easy! Easy! Open this do', man, I gotta talk!"

"Mouse?"

"Yeah, man! Lemme in!"

I snatched the door open with a curse on my lips but when I saw him I knew he'd changed again. He had on a plaid zoot

suit with Broadway suspenders and spats on his black
bluchers. He wore a silk hat and when he smiled you could
see the new gold rim and blue jewel on his front tooth. For
someone who never worked, Mouse knew how to keep himself in style.

"Man, what you doin' here this time'a night? I gotta work
in the mo'nin'!"

He pushed by me saying, "That's all right, Easy, I'ma buy
some'a yo' time this week." A tan rucksack hung from his
shoulder. I could hear the chink of bottles as it swung against
his side.

"We gotta talk, man," he said.

He led the way back into my apartment. All it was was a big
room with a Murphy bed. He sat down on the good chair and
I sat on the bed, facing him.

"Mouse, what do you . . ."

He held up his hand, half smiling like one of those saints in
the illustrated Bibles.

"Easy, I have got it."

He pulled Johnnie Walker from the sack.

"I have got it," he said. "Now do you got some glasses?
'Cause this here's Black Label and it won't do to swig it from
the neck."

"Man, what do you want?"

"I want some glasses, Easy, so we can celebrate my good
fortune. You the first one gonna know."

"Know what? All I know is I gotta get me some sleep."

"Then get me sumpin' t'drink wit' and I will deliver you the
potion of dreams."

There was no use in trying to argue when Mouse was in a

preaching mood. There were glasses in the closet at the back of the room. I rinsed them in a tub I kept back there.

"Jelly glasses?" Mouse turned up his nose while he poured. "Just . . . just . . . what do you want?"

He lay back in my stuffed chair and put his feet on my sheets. He flashed his new gold tooth at me and drank whiskey like it was water.

"You know I'm from down Pariah, Easy. Yes, sir! Just a country boy." He poured another glassful. "Down home, that's me."

I poured three fingers and waited. Mouse needed room to tell his story. He was afraid that the idea would get confused unless you had all the facts. If he was to tell you about a nail in a horse's foot he'd start off explaining coal and iron and how they make steel.

". . . an' you know us country boys is slow to get a idee, but once we got the picture we ain't never gonna let go. . . . You got a cigarette?"

"Got some papers an' shag."

"Uh-uh, no thanks. You know I cain't stand them leaves in my mouf." He twisted his lips and slugged back his second glass of scotch. "I guess you know I been kinda worried with the weddin' an' how me an' Etta ain't wit' much dough."

"Yeah, I know."

"Well, I got it all figgered out now." Mouse smiled so satisfied that I felt good.

But I said, "Com'on, man, it's midnight . . ."

"My stepdaddy."

"What?"

He looked at me real close then, like a dog does when a new smell comes by. Like he was wondering if I was food or foe or some love interest.

He said, "You like Etta, don't ya, Easy?"

"Yeah, sure I like her." I didn't like that question, though.

"Etta been hangin' out wit' us fo'years."

"Yeah, that's true," Mouse said, staring down into his jelly glass. Then he looked up at me. "But you like'er more'n just some friend. I mean, she's a good-lookin' woman, right?"

"She look fine. Now what's this about yo' stepdaddy?"

But he wouldn't let it go.

"She look good, but that's not what make her so fine. Etta ain't no bow-down woman, she stand up fo' what she want. An' no one better be foolin' wit' her 'less she like ya, 'cause Etta got a strong arm."

I laughed and said yeah but I was watching Mouse then. For all my size that small man scared me.

Mouse was laughing too, but his eyes were on mine.

"That's the truth," he said. "An' they ain't a real man who don't wonder what a powerful woman like that can do. 'Cause you know the first time I seen Etta sit down to a plate'a food I knew she was a hungry woman." He ran the length of his hand down his crotch. "Yeah, that Etta will eat you up!"

I poured out a little scotch and wondered if that was going to be my last drink.

He held my eye while he poured whiskey, while he drank. I could hear the house settling, it was so quiet.

"Why'ont you roll me one, Ease? You got the touch."

The pouch was on the end table, next to the knife. I reached for it slowly so he could see what I was doing.

I had to suck my tongue to get enough spit to wet the paper.

"Yeah. You know Etta wring me out and in the mo'nin' she tell me that if I wanna keep that good stuff fo'me I better do right." He laughed. "And she knew I had plenty'a women t'buy my clothes. An' I knew she weren't no virgin neither. . . . But I can understand a man, Easy." Mouse leaned back quickly and put his hand into his pocket.

I flinched and the tobacco and paper fell to the floor.

". . . a man," he continued as he came out with a red handkerchief to wipe his nose, "who run after a woman like that wit' his nose open an' his tongue hangin' down." I had been down in Galveston once when EttaMae lived there. I spent the night with her even though I knew she was Mouse's girl. He must've found out, but he couldn't know how bad I felt about it.

The next morning all Etta could talk about was how sweet a man Mouse was and how lucky I was to have him for a friend.

There I was facing a jealous fiancé when Etta had glazed over me like so much meat.

Mouse was smiling and I believe that he knew what I was thinking. I gave up trying to roll the cigarette; all I could do was stare at him and try not to look concerned.

SOMEBODY MIGHT WONDER why a big man like me would be scared of a small man, half his size. But size doesn't count for much in this world. I once saw Mouse put a knife in a big man's gut. I was drunk and that man, Junior Fornay was his name, was after me because he thought the girl I was with was his. He ripped off his shirt and came after me bare-fisted and bare-chested. They cleared the barroom and we went at it. But I was drunk and Junior was one of those field hands that you would swear was born from stone. He pounded me until I hit the floor and then he started kicking. I balled up to try and save myself but you know I could hear my dead mother that night: She was calling my name.

That's when Mouse strolled up.

Junior waved a piece of furniture at him but Mouse just put his hand in the air. I swear he couldn't reach as high as Junior's forehead but he said, "He got his lesson, man, you gotta let him live so he can learn."

"You better git . . ." was all Junior could say before Mouse had his stiletto buried, maybe just half an inch, in the field hand's gut. I was lying between them, looking up. I could see Mouse smiling and I could see Junior's face grow pale. Mouse quick-grabbed Junior's neck with his free hand and said, "You better drop that stick or I'ma stir the soup, boy."

I think I would rather have the beating than to see that, and smell it too.

SO I WAS LISTENING to Mouse with great respect.

". . . but you know, Easy, all that is past. I ain't the type'a man to bear no grudge. Po' men cain't afford no grudge. Shit! It's hard enough for a po' man t'get through the day."

He slapped my knee and leaned back in the chair. When he threw his leg over the armrest I knew I was safe.

"S-so, what 'bout yo' stepdaddy?" I asked.

"Yeah." Mouse stared at the ceiling with a smile. "You got that cigarette yet?"

I started rolling again.

"Yeah, my stepdaddy got a big pile'a money out on that farm somewhere. Big pile."

"He wanna give you some'a that?"

"Well, we ain't on the best terms—me an' Daddy Reese. You know he's a farm boy down t'his nuts an' he see everything like a farmer see his world. So when I come along he figgers I was the runt'a the litter and I should be put in a burlap sack and dumped in the river."

Mouse was smiling but he wasn't happy.

"Shoo, man! Even a farmer love his chirren."

"I ain't none'a his. My momma had me when she was still footloose an' feelin' good. Daddy Reese come nosin' around later."

"So how's that gonna help you and Etta?"

Mouse pulled up his pant leg, leaned forward, and slapped my knee again. He said, "That's just what I been thinkin', Easy. How one rich ole hick gonna help me when he cain't stand my face? I been thinkin' 'bout that fo' days. I go t'sleep thinkin' 'bout it an' then I wake up in the same frame'a mind.

"You know I went down to Galveston 'cause Etta wanted me t'see if I could get sumpin' down on the docks. Could you see me in that filthy water? Shit! But I went down there because you gotta respect yo' woman."

That was Mouse to a word. Children loved him and their mothers did too.

"I was down on the docks eatin' a sandwich and watchin'

the boys down there. They had this game they played. You
see, in the hot day them ship rats crawl up on the top'a the
pilin's to git some sun. They just lay out in the sun an' bake
with they long nekked tails hangin' down an' wavin' 'round
the logs. Uh! It's disgustin'. But anyway, them boys sneak up
to where the rats is an' they wait real quiet right next to the
tail."

Mouse sat up straight and clapped his hands like a gunshot.

"Then they grab the tail an' swing that rat through the air
till it smash on the pier! Oh, man, that was sumpin'! I watched
'em do that fo' a long time. Shoot, they musta killed twenty'a
them things. . . . Then I caught a ride on a vegetable truck
comin' back t'Houston. I was still thinkin' 'bout them boys,
when it hit me. You know I kept thinkin' that those boys
couldn't hesitate a minute 'cause that rat is ready t'bite the
first thing you touch'im, an' you know the on'y thing worse
than a rat bite is a man bite."

Mouse sat back, showing his teeth.

I handed him the cigarette and he lit it up. He lay back and
took a deep draw.

It looked like he was through talking, so I asked, "So what,
man? What you gonna do 'bout the money?"

"I'ma go up to Pariah an' get it, that's what."

"How you gonna do that?"

"I don't know, Easy. All I can tell ya is that I ain't gonna
hesitate one minute."

Mouse wanted something from me, and he wanted me to
ask him what that something was. But I was too stubborn to
give in to that.

So he puffed on his cigarette and I fumbled around with

my glass. When he'd look at me I'd just look back. Mouse had light gray eyes.

Finally he said, "So, Easy, what you workin' at now?"

"Gardenin' for the Lewis fam'ly. They man is sick."

"You know how t'drive a car, right?"

"Yeah."

"I tell you what. I give ya fifteen dollars t'drive me to Pariah fo'a couple' a days."

"Shit!"

"Yeah, man, I ain't lyin'."

"Let's see it."

Mouse got that wary dog look again and said in a quiet voice, "I ain't never asked you t'prove nuthin', Easy."

I knew right then that he wanted to trade; that he'd forget about me and Etta if I'd drive him to Pariah for a fifteen-dollar IOU. That's how Mouse was, he didn't care about me and his woman; the only thing that ever got Mouse mad was if you played with his money or caught him in a lie. This was just business, plain and simple.

"What kinda car you got?"

" 'Thirty-six Ford. Drive so smooth you think you was in a boat."

"Now where you gonna get a car like that an' you don't even drive?"

"Otum Chenier want me t'take care of it while he gone down Lake Charles." Mouse grinned and rubbed his chin. "Seem like one'a his folks is sick."

"And when you wanna go?" I asked.

"Maybe half hour 'fore dawn."

"Tomorrah?"

"Com'on, Ease. It's late. I got business down south an' I'ma pay you fo'it too. I ain't got no time t'waste."

"I got a job, man."

"Easy, you work fo'them three weeks an' you be lucky t'get fifteen dollars. Soon as they man is back you know they gonna put yo' butt out. An' I got food, an' whiskey, an' gas money. I know ev'ry pretty girl in Pariah. An', man, Etta deserve a good weddin', 'cause you know she sumpin' else." He winked at that.

I wanted to go. I knew it from the minute he yelled in my door. I was a young man then, barely nineteen years old, and alone in the world. Mouse was my only real friend, and even though he was crazy and wild I knew he cared for me—in his way. He made me mad sometimes but that's what good friends and family do.

I wasn't mad because Mouse had won Etta. I was mad because when they got married I was going to lose my friend to his wife and family. This was going to be the last time we would go running in the streets together. I'd've gone with him without the threats and the IOU.

"I want my fifteen dollars, man," I said. "You know I ain't doin' this fo'my health."

"Don't you worry 'bout a thing, Easy. We both git sumpin' outta this."

MOUSE WAS CURLED UP in my secondhand upholstered chair like a little boy. The room was all kinds of gray from light that leaked in through the torn shades and the cracks in the door. He fell asleep as soon as the light went out, but I woke up then. I lay there in the dark thinking about the time Mouse had saved my life.

I remembered Junior holding his bloody shirt and running from the bar. Then I thought of what Mouse had said when I tried to thank him.

"Shit, man, I din't save you. I just wanted to cut that boy 'cause he think he so bad.... See what he think now...." And we never talked about it again.

CHAPTER

2

EARLY MORNING IS THE BEST TIME. You're fully
rested but not awake enough to remember how hard it
all is. Morning is like being a child again, and morning before
the sun is out is like those magic times that you hid under the
bed and in between the clothes hanging in your mother's
closet. Times when any kind of miracle could come about just
as normal as a spider making her web.

I remember waking up in the dark once when I was very
small. I jumped right out of bed and went up next to the
screen door on the back porch to see what kind of fantastic
thing was going on outside. At first I couldn't see anything, but
there was a clopping sound, nickering, and a deep voice that
made me feel calm and wondering. Slowly, coming out from
the darkness, I saw a gray shimmering next to a tall black pillar. The shimmer turned into a big horse and the pillar
became my father holding out an apple and cooing in his bass

voice, "Ho! Yeah, boy," even though the horse was tame and eating from his hand.

I drifted into sleep thinking that we were poor and didn't own a horse. When I woke up it was light and there was no horse to be seen. I asked my father about it but he told me that I was dreaming—where were poor people like us going to find big gray stallions?

But there were horse chips behind the barn, and hoof-prints too.

I decided that it was a magic horse and man that I'd seen. From that day on I believed that magic hides in the early morning. If you get up early enough you might find something so beautiful that it would be all right if you just died right then because nothing else in life could ever be better.

IT WAS STILL DARK when we made it down to Lucinda Greg's house. She was Otum Chenier's girlfriend. I warmed up the engine while Mouse changed clothes and made lunch inside. He came out in gray pants and a gray shirt, work clothes that fit him like dress clothes.

When we drove off it was still way before dawn. Mouse was sleeping against the passenger door and I was driving with the few feeble lights of Houston behind us. It was going to be a warm day but the air still held a light chill of night. I wanted to sing but I didn't because Mouse wouldn't have understood my feelings about magic and the morning. So I just drove quietly, happy on that flat Texas road.

People don't understand southern Texas. They think that the land there is ugly and flat. They take their opinion about the land and put it on the people—but they're wrong on both counts. If they could see Texas in the early dawn like I saw it that day they would know a Texas that is full of potential from the smallest rock to the oldest woman on the farm.

The road wasn't paved or landscaped. On either side there were dense shrubs and bushes with knotty pines and cherry and pear trees scattered here and there. I was especially aware of the magnolias, their flowers looking like white faces staring down from shadow.

They say it's like a desert down there, and they're right—at least sometimes. There are stretches of land that have hardly anything growing, but even then it's no simple story. Texas is made up of every kind of soil; there's red clay and gray sod and fertile brown, shipped in or strained over by poor farmers trying to make the land work. That earth gives you the feeling of confidence because it's so much and so different and, mainly, because it's got the patience to be there not ever having to look for a better place.

But there's no such thing as a desert down near the Gulf. The rains come to make bayous and swamps and feed every kind of animal and bird and varmint.

As the night disappeared the last foxes and opossums made their way to shelter. Animals everywhere were vanishing with the shadows; field mice and some deer, foxes, rabbits, and skunk.

"I'ma show you how t'fish while we down here, Ease."

I jumped when Mouse spoke.

"Man, ain't nuthin' you could tell me. I been droppin' my line in the water since before I could talk."

"That's all right," he said with a sneer. "But I show you how the master fish."

He took a fried egg sandwich from a brown paper sack and tore it in half.

"Here you go."

We were both quiet as the sun filled in the land with light. To me it was like the world was growing and I was happy to be on that road.

After a while I asked Mouse how it was that he happened to get Otum's car just when he needed a ride.

Mouse smiled and looked humble. "You know Otum's a Cajun, an' them Cajuns is fam'ly down to the bone. They'd kill over a insult to their blood that normal folks like you an' me would just laugh at. An' Otum is a real Cajun. That's a fact."

Mouse knew how to tell you a story. It was like he was singing a song and the words were notes going up and down the scales, even rhyming when it was right. He'd turn phrases that I wanted to use myself but it seemed that I couldn't ever get the timing right. Sometimes what he said fit so perfectly I couldn't ever find the right time to say it again.

". . . I always known that a message from his momma would light a fire under Otum. An' puttin' out fires is my especiality." We laughed at that. "So that night I come home from Galveston I stayed over at Lucinda's, for a weddin' gift she said. I thought 'bout how she take care'a Otum's car an' how they got a phone down at that beauty shop she work for. . . ."

Mouse smiled with all his teeth and put his foot against the dashboard so he could sit back comfortably. "You know once Otum got that message from Lucinda he knew he couldn't take his car down there. The bayou ain't no place t'drive no good car. So Lucinda tole him that you would start it up for him and look in on it every once an' a while."

"Me?"

"Well, yeah, it had t'be you, Easy. I cain't drive no car. Anyway, Otum never did trust me too much."

WE HAD BEEN GOING SOUTHEAST for close to two hours when we saw two people with thumbs out on the road. A big young man and a girl, maybe fifteen, with a healthy chest and smile.

"Pull on over, Ease," Mouse said. "Let's pick 'em up."

"You know 'em?" I asked as we passed by.

"Uh-uh, but oppu'tunity is ev'rywhere an' I ain't passin' up no bets."

"Man, you don't know what they's up to. They could be robbers fo'all you know."

"If they is then this here gonna be they last stand."

I shifted the clutch down and put on the brake.

As soon as we stopped, Mouse was out with the door open and the seat folded up. He waved at the couple and they came running. The boy was dragging a duffel bag that was bigger than his girlfriend.

"Come on!" Mouse shouted. "Jump in the back wit' me, man. 'Cause Easy got all kindsa dirty rags back here an' you don't want no girl in that."

"That's all right. We sit together," the young man said in a gruff tone.

"Uh-uh, Clifton," the girl complained in a high voice. "I don't wanna get filthy! Go'on an sit back there wit' him. You can still see me."

Mouse smiled and gestured for the boy to get in. Clifton did as he was asked to do, but he wasn't happy about it.

I could see in his face that Clifton hadn't had a happy day in his life. His jaw was set and his eyes were hard but he couldn't have been over seventeen. He was what Mouse called "a truly poor man." Someone who doesn't have a thing and is so mad about it that he isn't likely to ever get anything.

"Where you-all goin'?" I asked.

"Down t'N'Orleans," the girl said. She looked in my eyes to see how surprised and jealous I'd be. She had a wide face and a forehead that sloped back. Her eyes were so far apart it looked as if she couldn't focus both of them on the same thing. Her look was careless and lazy, and I looked away before I got myself into trouble.

"Where you people from?" Mouse asked in his friendliest tone.

"Nowhere special," Clifton mumbled. "Where you-all goin'?"

"Pariah," Mouse announced. "Farmin' capital of south Texas."

"Hm!" The girl frowned. "I ain't never even heard'a that place." She turned her back to the door and put her bare feet on the seat, her toes grazing my leg.

"What's your name?" I asked as I shifted gears.

"Ernestine." She showed me her full set of teeth. "What's yours?"

"They call me Easy, an' they call him Mouse."

She laughed and dug her toes under my thigh. "Them ain't even names at all. What's yo' real name?"

I never liked telling strangers my real name, but with her toes wiggling under my leg and Clifton breathing down my neck I didn't feel like arguing.

"Ezekiel."

She guffawed at that and got her whole foot under my thigh. I had a hard time keeping the car in the road.

While we rode along Ernestine flirted with me in the front seat and Clifton pouted in the back. Mouse was telling us a story about how a bad man in Houston shot his foot off while trying to shoot Mouse. It was a funny story and we all laughed, even Clifton, in that respectful way you're supposed to laugh when complimenting a well-told lie. But I knew that Mouse wasn't lying. That gangster, fat Joe Withers, died from gangrene poison. He had made the mistake of grabbing EttaMae one night and we all knew that Mouse would get him one day.

Ernestine was still giggling and wiggling her toes when Mouse started checking Clifton out.

"Ain't I seen you wit' a guitar down in Fifth Ward? I swear I seen a big man like you down there playin'."

"Ain't me, man. I ain't the least bit musical."

"Well, yeah, I guess you must know. It's just I seen this boy who looked powerful like you and I wondered why such a big man would waste his time on music."

"I cain't tell ya. I mean I like t'listen but, uh, you know, I ain't never gonna play nuthin'."

"Uh-huh." I could see Mouse nod in the mirror. "That's just how I feel. You know I go on down t' George's saloon an' get all the music I needs. You ever go there?"

"Naw. The way them men in the bars an' juke joints be lookin' at Ernestine gets me mad." Clifton talked slowly as if every word he said had to be exactly right.

Ernestine stopped wagging her foot long enough to say, "He just jealous, that's all. 'Cause the men like a girl wit' big titties like I got." She sneered at him; Mouse and I looked away.

"You shouldn't be talkin' like that, honey. What these men gonna think?"

"Well I am nice t'look at, ain't I, 'Zekiel?" she said as she arched her foot.

I swear that I meant to look out at the road but I found myself staring down at her. Clifton would have opened my head if he saw my eyes but I guess he was too busy looking at her to notice what I was doing.

"Ernestine, stop it!"

"I will not! I will not! On'y reason we here is 'cause you so jealous an' you don't know that a girl can get a compliment an' not do nuthin' 'bout it!"

"That's enough now, girl!" Clifton was threatening but Ernestine didn't care.

"What difference it make? If that boy die you know they gonna fines you an' they gonna get you too!"

Mouse had a talent; he could smile without letting it show. You could be looking at him and if you didn't know it you'd think his face was just plain, but if you knew what to look for you'd see how his eyes got larger and how his mouth lost its hardness.

He was smiling then.

"You in some kinda trouble, Clifton?" Mouse spoke the boy's name like they'd known each other for years.

"Ain't nuthin', man. Just a little disagreement."

Ernestine frowned and turned to look out at the road. I missed her toes under my leg.

"I wanna know, man, 'cause we here wichyou in the car an' if the po-lice stops us I just wanna know," Mouse said.

Clifton didn't say a word.

"You know you can get in trouble wit' the law fo'just he'pin' somebody done done sumpin' wrong. . . ." Mouse let that one hang for a minute, then he said, "An' you know a guilty man more nekked than a baby, the patrols see you out here. . . . I mean I wouldn't wanna put you out or nuthin', but me an' Easy cain't afford no close look by John Law ourselfs. . . ."

"Ain't nuthin'," Clifton said again. "Man was lookin' at Ernestine wit'out no respect an' I showed him a little sumpin', that's all."

"He beat that boy so bad that he prob'ly dead!" Ernestine shouted with her lips stuck straight out.

"Is that true, Clifton?"

"He wasn't movin' much when we lefted," the sullen boy admitted. "But that don't mean he dead."

"Anybody see it?"

"We was in a bar fulla people!" Ernestine had turned completely around. She was like a little girl in that dirty blue dress with little pictures of cows stamped all over it.

Mouse shook his head and hummed his dissatisfaction, "Mmmmmm-mm! An' you out here in the road for any hick sheriff t'haul you in? Mm! You two headed fo'a rope."

"I tried t'tell 'im," Ernestine said. "But he won't listen t'me. He think he so smart an' they gonna hang him."

"You ain't gonna be too frisky in jail neither," Mouse answered.

"What you mean? I ain't done nuthin'!"

"But you wit' a bad man. The law see you wit' him an' they call you the same. An' if you a woman they call you a bad man's girl—an' that's even worse."

Ernestine pouted and turned to put her face against the window. Clifton hunched down in his seat and glowered. And Mouse sat back with his plain face secretly grinning from ear to ear.

I started thinking about my magic horse and how far away he was. It was closing in on noon and there wasn't a shred of my morning left.

We drove for a little while in silence. The land was getting more lush as we pressed south into bayou country. Our passengers were brooding and Mouse was waiting; waiting for them to accept his wisdom.

Finally he said, "Look, kids, I know you got troubles an' I ain't tryin t'be no bad man to ya. It's just that I know what's goin' on. . . . But me an' Easy got a heart." Ernestine turned her face to him, reminding me of a flower being drawn to the sun. "An' we wanna he'p ya, right, Ease?" I didn't say a word, but that didn't bother him. "Now listen: You cain't stay on the road, 'cause that's where the po-lice be lookin'. An' you cain't stop out here, 'cause country folk is suspicious'a strangers an' anyway, if Ernestine let sumpin' slip like she just did, then you in it deep. So what you kids need is a place where they gonna look out fo'you. What you need is Momma Jo."

"Who?" That was me.

"Friend'a mine, Ease. Momma Jo. They call her a witch an' she be 'lone most the time. If we bring her a strong man an' pretty girl she be one happy woman."

"But I thought you said that these country people ain't got time for strangers?"

"True, true. But I ain't no stranger. I been bringin' homemade an' store-bought liquor t'Momma Jo fo'years. She trust anybody I brang."

"But why you wanna he'p us?" Clifton asked.

"It's a favor, man. Maybe you he'p me someday." That time Mouse smiled for real.

"Uh-uh, I don't think so. We plan t'go out t'Looziana t'my folks," Clifton said.

"You done kilt a boy an' you gonna hang that on yo' folks' neck?"

"That's across state line, they cain't do nuthin' down there."

"An' you don't think the white man gonna be down there? You don't think that if he know you at your momma's that he cain't go get you?"

"How anybody gonna know where I am—'less you tell 'em?"

"Boy, you better get that chip offa yo' shoulder an' listen t'me." Mouse sat back and frowned. "Now the first thing is that the cops know your name. I know that 'cause Ernestine was there an' she love t'yell 'Clifton.' Second thing is they know you headed fo' the state line 'cause that's where a man scared'a the law always be headed. An' last thing is they know you gonna go whey it's safe, an' seein that you already wit' yo' girlfriend they know you gonna go see Momma. . . . The man ain't no fool, Clifton."

Mouse actually scared me. I was amazed and proud of him. He revealed to us the police mind in a way that I never even considered. I could see in the mirror that Clifton felt the same way.

"Com'on, Clifton," Ernestine pleaded. "Let's do it. He right 'bout these country cops."

Clifton didn't say anything. The only change in him at all was that his jaw set a little tighter.

Mouse tapped my shoulder and said, "When you see a ole beat-up sign that say Rag Bayou, follah it."

The turnoff to Rag Bayou was rough and unpaved. We bounced along. Everyone was quiet. Everyone was lost in their thoughts. I kept thinking about that horse in the backyard and how it got there. I was five when I first saw it, and then, fourteen years later, it came to me, from nowhere it seemed, that my daddy had stolen that horse and sold it for meat.

3

A MIST OF GNATS AND MOSQUITOES swarmed along the road. Mouse was shouting over the whining cicadas, "Turn down there, Easy! . . . That's it! . . . Take a lef'! . . ." The path was so rutted that I worried about breaking an axle—and I knew Otum loved that car more than his whole Cajun family.

"You can stop it right here, man!" Mouse yelled at last.

"We in the middle'a the road, fool! I gotta park."

"Okay." He shrugged. "But Otum ain't gonna like his Ford knee deep in swamp."

"But we cain't leave it in the road. What they gonna do when they come drivin' down here?"

Mouse laughed. "Man who gonna drive down here but a fool?"

I wished I had an answer to that. I pulled the car as far over to the side of the road as I could, and hoped that there was enough space in case some other fool decided to drive by.

"Com'on, Clifton, you safe fo'the first time since you laid that boy down," Mouse said.

"Hey, man." Clifton put up his hands. "Keep it quiet."

Mouse smiled and followed Ernestine out of the car door. Clifton went too.

But I stayed in the car putting on my heavy shirt and pulling my cotton cap down to my ears.

Mouse leaned in the window and said, "What you doin', Easy?"

"It's them bugs," I said. "Just one mosquito in a room will bite me twenty times and every bite swells up into a hump on my skin, and every hump itches me until I scratch it hard enough to draw blood. I hate bugs."

"You just too sweet an' sensitive," Mouse said. "All I gotta do is wave my hand in front'a my face once or twice and the bugs leave me be. An' if anything bite me he ain't never gonna bite nuthin' else."

I came out finally. Mouse slapped my shoulder and said, "Right this way, honey boy."

We walked into a wall of vines and baby bamboo. It was reedy and mulchy and thick with gnats. It was hot too. Ernestine squealed every time a frog jumped or one of those bright red swamp birds got startled and croaked its hoarse swampsong. I was sweating heavy in all those clothes and still getting bites on my face and hands.

"How far is it?" I yelled over the cicadas.

"It's up here, Ease."

"How far?"

"I'ont rightly know, man." He smiled and let go of a bamboo stalk.

"What you mean you don't know?" I had to duck down to keep the bamboo from hitting me in the face.

"Ole Momma Jo's a witch, an' witch houses out here is like boats." He made his voice sound ghostly. "Floatin' on the bayou."

He didn't believe in that voodoo stuff, but Clifton and Ernestine got quiet and looked around as if they expected to see Baron Samedi looking out from under his skull mask.

"You can tell you gettin' close t'Momma's when the cicadas stop singin' an' the mosquitoes die down," Mouse said.

I thought he was still trying to scare us, but after a while there came a sweet wood-burnt scent. Soon after that the whining of the cicadas receded and the ground became firmer.

We came to a clearing and Mouse said, "Here we is," but all I saw was a stand of stunted pear trees with a big avocado rising up behind them.

"She live in the open?" Clifton asked.

A cloud shifted and the sun shone between two pear trunks. A light glinted from the trees. Mouse whistled a shrill warbled note and in a while the door came open.

It was a house hidden by trees way out there.

The house was a shock, but it was the woman standing there that scared me.

She was tall, way over six feet, wearing a short, light blue dress that was old and faded. Over her dress was a wide white apron; her jet-black skin shone against those pale colors so brightly that I winced when I first saw her. She was strongly built with wide shoulders and big strong legs.

When she strode toward us I noticed the cudgel in her

broad fist. For the first time in my life I felt the roots of my hair tingle. She came to within three strides of us and pushed her handsome face forward like something wild sniffing at strangers. There was no sympathy in her face. Ernestine jumped behind Clifton and I took a step back.

Then she smiled. Big pure yellow teeth that were all there and healthy.

"Raymond!" The swamp behind us got even quieter. "Raymond, boy it's good, good to see you." She lifted Mouse by his shoulders and hugged him to her big bosom.

"Mmmmmmmmmmmmmm-mm, it's good." She put him down and beamed on him like a smiling black sun. "Raymond," she said. "It's been too long, honey."

Raymond is Mouse's real name, but nobody except EttaMae called him that.

"Jo, I brung you some store-bought." He held out the sack that still had two fifths of Johnnie Walker. "An' some guests." He waved his hand at us.

Momma Jo's teeth went away but she was still smiling when she asked, "These friends?"

"Oh yeah, Momma. This here is Easy Rawlins. He's my best friend. An' these chirren is the victims of a po-lice hunt. They in love too."

She took the sack and said, "Com'on then, let's get in."

We followed her in between the trees into the house, passing from day into night. The room was dark like nighttime because the sun couldn't make it through the leaves to her windows. It was a big room lit by oil lanterns. The floor was cool soil that was swept and dry. The whole place was cool as if the trees soaked up all the swamp heat. In a corner two small armadillos were snuffling over corncobs and above them was a pure white cat, its hair standing on end as it hissed at us.

The cat was on a ledge over a fireplace. Also on the ledge were thirteen skulls. Twelve of them were long-snout opossums, six on either side of a human skull that had been dried with the skin still on it. The skull leaned back with its teeth pushed forward, dried black lips for gums. The teeth were brown but here and there white bone poked through cracked human leather. The eyelids were shut and sunken but there was no repose in the broad features of that face. It was as if the agony of life had followed that poor soul into the afterworld.

"Domaque," Momma Jo said, and I turned to see her looking at me.

"What?"

"My husband," she said. "Com'on, chirren, have a seat." She gestured for us to settle on the dirty blankets and piles of pillows she had surrounding the fireplace. There were only two pieces of wood furniture in the whole room. A three-legged stool and a rough-hewn plank table that had six legs. The table was piled with dried plants and all kinds of powders in glass jars and bowls. I didn't look too close at the table because I didn't want to see any other keepsakes like Domaque.

She opened the sack and smiled when she saw little Johnnie. She said to Mouse, "You brought me lightnin'," then she looked at me, "an' sugah."

"That's right, Momma, you know I take care'a you."

"Uh-uh, baby, you takes care'a Raymond, an' that's why I loves you." Momma laughed. "Yes, yes. Raymond take care'a hisself. . . ."

We settled in and Momma broke out the scotch with hand-carved wood bowls that she used for glasses. She poured us each a drink, and then another one. We were down to the bottom of the second bottle. Mouse was talking about the wedding when Momma turned to Clifton and asked, "An' why is the po-lice chasin' you, honey?"

"Well they ain't really aftah me at all. Just sumpin' come up an' me an' Ernestine had ta go, that's all."

Momma Jo had been smiling and pleased the whole time, but she frowned then.

"He kilt a boy in a bar fight, Momma," Mouse said. And before Clifton could speak, "Momma don't always know what's truf, Clifton, but she sure'n hell can smell a lie."

Ernestine was staring up at Momma's face like she had never seen anything like her. "Tell'er, Clift," she said. "She ain't gonna hurt us."

"You just trust ev'rybody, huh, girl? I might as well go on back there an' give up, huh?"

"No!"

Momma Jo smiled and said, "Com'on, honey, you tell me the truth an' I he'p." Those yellow teeth against her face and the armadillo spoor brought to mind a bear in her dark den. She seemed wild and violent and I could feel my heart working.

"She the best chance you got," Mouse told him.

I didn't say anything. I knew that Mouse was working those kids for his own purposes but I didn't care. I was just a driver, a cabbie waiting for his fare.

Clifton was fair-minded, you could see that by the way he worried over the pressure those three put on him. He was sullen and sulky but his arms and shoulders were jerking so that you knew that the story wanted to come out.

Mouse poured him another scotch and Clifton busted open like an overripe melon.

He told Momma the same story he told in the car; he used the same words exactly. I knew right then that Clifton couldn't lie to save his life.

It was a strange day. That house was always midnight with its oil lamps burning and the armadillos and the cat skirting the edges of the room. Mouse was slouched up against the wall staring at the dead fireplace as if it were raging. Clifton was looking into his lap and Ernestine had her eyes glued to Momma Jo.

Jo was taking it all in. She looked at each one in his turn. But when she looked at me she'd catch my eye and smile so it seemed like that old witch was flirting. She was more than twice my age but she was still a handsome woman without a wrinkle on her fine-featured face. And I knew that in women it's the face that gets old first.

She was sitting on the stool with her legs crossed like a man, it was only that long white apron that kept her modest. She was smoking a hand-rolled cigarette for a long time before she said, "You chirren got two thangs to do. First off you gotta hide while they look fo'you. That is if that boy really is dead. But that's easy, 'cause you kin stay here. I could use a strong boy like Clifton and Ernestine can help me wit' my herbs.

"But you got a worse thing 'cause Clifton cain't satisfy this young girl's womanly needs an' she ain't woman enough t'teach him yet."

"Wha?" Clifton was drunk by then so he staggered to his

feet to challenge the witch. Clifton was a big boy, about my height with more heft to him, but Momma Jo had him by a head and twenty pounds.

She stood up to his face and said, "Sit'own, boy."

And he did.

"I ain't worried 'bout yo' pride, honey. You can see that Ernestine is out tryin t'make men appreciate what she got. That's 'cause she want sumpin'. She want satisfaction."

Ernestine started crying.

Mouse had that invisible smile across his face.

"I can he'p you chirren," Momma said. "I got a powder bring out what's sleepin' in you, make you see each other a whole new way."

She went to her table and started working with her powders and spoons. Mouse crawled over and nudged my arm. "Oh this gonna be a gem, Easy," he whispered. "Momma Jo's especiality is love."

"But what's this gotta do wit' yo' stepdaddy?"

"I'ont know, but it's lookin' good," he said. "Aftah while I'ma go out t'see a friend. Don't you be worried though."

"I go wichyou."

"Uh-uh, Easy. These country folks don't like crowds too much."

Right then Momma Jo interrupted, "Ezekiel? Honey, reach over on that shelf and bring me that blue jug. Yeah, that's it. Bring it over here, baby. Now, Clifton an' Ernestine, you-all bring me yo' cups."

She poured a strong alcohol liquid into their bowls and then carefully measured some powder and dried leaves into each one. Clifton got a brown powder and Ernestine a white.

"Now drink it all down at once, don't leave nuthin' in the cup . . . yeah, that's it."

They did what she said like they were children. But I didn't question it either, because that's how life was back then. You listened to older folks and did what you were told. Even if you knew better you'd follow the rules because that's how we were raised. Everybody but Mouse.

Mouse never took an order unless that's what he wanted to do. Mouse wasn't the only man I knew who'd stand up for what he believed, but he was different in one way: Most men who stood up for themselves would rather die than be slaves; Mouse would've rather killed.

"Okay, babies," Momma said to Ernestine and Clifton. "You go sit together next to the hearth. Ezekiel baby? Why don't you blow out some'a them lights an' I tell you all a story."

4

I WENT AROUND THE BIG ROOM blowing out lamps. It became more nighttime than ever but I knew it was afternoon not ten yards from where we sat.

Momma Jo brought her stool in front of us and looked down on the two lovers.

"How you chirren feelin'?"

"Fine," they said together.

Clifton had softened with the drink. I think he felt better too, once he told Jo his story. Good men always need to confess.

"That's good," she said. "You was lookin' at my husband, huh, 'Zekiel?"

I felt her attention burning on me even though she was looking at them.

"What husband?" I asked.

"That's him up on the mantel place," she said, nodding at

the row of skulls. "I met him more'n twenny-three years ago. I'as just a girl, hardly in my teens. He was a big man with a great big laugh and powerful arms. Ev'rything about Domaque was big."

A shiver ran through Ernestine.

"But the biggest thing about him was his heart," Momma Jo continued. "He loved chirren an' animals an' trees an' even dirt. He used to say that he wanted everybody to know him an' he wanted to get to know ev'rybody he could.

"If a man had a job to do and it was too much for him, he'd call on Domaque an' that job was done. Dom didn't ask fo'-money or barter or anything; if you give him somethin' he was glad t'take it and if you couldn't pay, well, Dom knew what it was like t'be poor too."

The lovers were frozen like startled deer. But every once in a while Ernestine shook.

Momma Jo flashed her yellow teeth and said, "Well, you know it's the same old story over and over again. I was a big girl fo'my age. Matter'a fact I was bigger'n most women by the time I was thirteen, and womanly too. My parents wanted t'fool themselves that I was still a chile, but when I saw Dom my li'l dolls fell away. When I see him an' hear him laugh, 'cause he was always ready t'laugh, I'd just swell up inside so it felt like the clothes was gonna split right off me.

"You know Dom knew ev'ry fam'ly to a child fo'twenty miles 'round Pariah. He did work on ev'ry farm an' backyard we got here but he kept findin' excuses to be 'round our place. Dom was what we called a rover. He slept wherever he could in trade fo'labor. He worked a lot at the Fontanot place next to ours or at the Hollis farm down the road. And ev'ry chance he got he'd drop by t'say hi t'Daddy, but you know his eyes was on my woman's body in that little girl's dress.

"My titties stuck straight out when I'as a girl." She looked me in the eye when she said that.

"Fin'ly one day I got t'get away down to the Hollis place when Dom was workin' to pull a stump from their field. I go down there with some bread an' sausage an' I told him 'bout a place where we could eat. An' when we get t'my li'l hideaway in the trees I hand him the paper bag an' then pull my dress off. That's all I could think about. I stripped down an' looked at him. An' do you know that big man went limp on the ground just like a sack'a bones. I shoulda seen somethin' was wrong right then but before I got a chance he come over me like a tidal wave." She frowned, remembering pain and pleasure at the same time. "He got me on my back and on my knees; he made me ride'im like a horse. And once he got in me he didn't want out, uh-uh. I was sore and raw and bloody but Domaque kept comin'. When I fin'ly couldn't hold back and started t'cry he got up an' said, 'Gimme that sausage,' an' I thought he was through an' had t'eat. But he scooped up the fat that hardened in the paper an' rubbed it on his thing. Then he started slippin' in an' outta me like a fish. . . . You know they put spices in that sausage an' it burns ya if you got a cut. Yeah. . . ."

Clifton had his hand on his crotch and Ernestine hugged her chest but they didn't touch each other. They looked like tired children, about to throw a fit.

"That was Domaque. First he taught me how men hurts women and then he started t'cry. He was afraid 'bout how my daddy would have to fight ovah what happened. Seem like Domaque had a wife down in Looziana so he couldn't do right

by me and he liked my daddy so he didn't want t'kill'im." She
sat back and took a draw on her cigarette. Momma Jo's face
was handsome and hard, almost like a man's face but you
could see she was a woman. "I got a room behind that blanket,
Ernestine. Anytime you want you an' Clifton can go on back
there."

Ernestine was pushing a small homemade pillow down
between her legs but she shook her head, no.

"So he ran off." Momma shifted over to me. "He come out
here when they wasn't nobody in the swamp and he built this
house. And as soon as it was good enough t'sleep in he come
an' got me. I din't wanna go but he needed me so bad that
what I felt din't seem t'mattah. He took me out here and he
started callin' me a witch. He said that I had spelled him an' he
had t'have me, an' he did too. Ev'ry night he'd come out here
his pants was halfway down by the time he was in the do'. At
first I liked it but then it got to be too much, too much. . . ."

"Uh!" Ernestine had her hand down the front of Clifton's
pants, pulling back and forth, hard; I didn't know if he called
out in pleasure or pain.

"You chirren better go on back now. Go on, get in there
behind the blanket," Momma Jo said, and she walked across
the room to pull the blanket back for them. Clifton staggered
like a drunk with Ernestine pulling on his dick, she tried to
hide what she was doing, but you could tell.

When the blanket swung down they started making love
noises. I was on my feet and headed for the front door when
Momma touched my arm.

"Oh yeah, Clifton!" came Ernestine's voice from the other
room.

Momma Jo said, "Come sit'own wit' me, Daddy. Over here."

I looked over to where Mouse had been sitting but he was gone. There was no sign of my friend. I remembered that he planned to see someone. I wondered if he planned to leave me in that house.

"Com'on, sit'own, Daddy." Jo was leaning back on a pile of pillows, pulling on my thigh. Ernestine was yelling in short coughs. The armadillos wrestled in the corner. I got weak and fell to my knees.

"I ain't finished my story yet." She put her arms around me and rested my head back against her shoulder. I was too dizzy to fight her.

"Oooooo-uh!" The voice was so twisted I couldn't tell if it was Ernestine or Clifton.

"You wanted t'know how Dom's head came t'be here, din't you?" Jo's whisper smelled of tobacco and whiskey, of garlic and sweet chili. When she laid her hand on my thing I realized it was hard.

"I cut it off myself," she said on a slender breath.

Ernestine had settled down into long breathing sighs that cut into the room like hot spoons into lard, but I didn't pay much attention. My stomach had started churning. I was sure that I was going to vomit, but Momma Jo put her big hand against my chest and pressed, then released, then pressed.

She said, "Shhhh, baby. Be quiet now," so softly that I could barely hear her over Ernestine.

I lay there and let her breathe for me. I could feel her heart pounding from a vein throbbing in her thigh against my leg. Ernestine was chanting Clifton's name over and over. Momma

Jo's hand was pressing down and letting go. I closed my eyes, wishing my mind back home.

"My daddy s'pected Domaque of takin' me," she said. "An' Dom was worried. He brought a old woman he called his auntie out t'take care'a me 'cause he din't come out too much, he was so scared that one'a Daddy's friends would catch on. An' Luvia, that was his auntie, started t'teach me about herbs an' other things."

"That how you become a witch?" My voice cracked; there was the taste of bile in my throat.

"It was Domaque made me a witch."

"Oh-ohhhhh," Ernestine softly sighed.

Momma Jo pressed my chest, then she moved her hand down over my belly to press my thing; then she pressed my chest again. She did that over and over while she said:

"Then one day Daddy shot 'im. He got tired'a waitin' an' he shot Dom down. He came after Dom with a shotgun fulla buckshot. He tole Dom t'bring me back but Dom turned his back an' started walkin'. He din't say nuthin'; not where I was or if he had taken me. An' Daddy kilt 'im. Luvia tole me about it an' she got his body an' brung it out here t'me. She knew how wild Dom was fo'me, she knew how Dom died rather than t'hurt my daddy. She said that if I kept a piece'a that love wit' me then I'd be powerful an' my baby would be healthy, male, an' strong."

She worked her hand down into my pants as Ernestine spoke my mind from behind the curtain.

"I cut off his head an' put it in a barrel'a salt fo' five years. Dom Jr. was born an' Luvia passed on. Daddy died." She squeezed me hard when she said that. "An' here we is. . . ."

Her kisses were salty and thick.

*   *   *

WHAT I REMEMBER MOST are the smells: her mouth and
her musky armpits, the strong smell that almost burned from
between her legs. Her feet smelled like earth along with the
weak scent of manure. She tasted of salt. And after Ernestine
quieted down, the only sound was the deep breathing and the
rise and fall of Momma Jo's body. The sound filled the room
like God watching from some dark corner.

I didn't want to do it but Momma Jo was strong; she
clenched her arms and legs around me so powerfully that my
"No" was crushed down to "Yes." She whispered in my ear what
she wanted and I lost my mind for a while; lost it to her desire.

After a long while I found myself pressing down hard on
her and yelling something, but I can't remember what it was. I
felt pain in my head and realized that she was pulling my hair.
She was yelling too, "You done, Easy! It's over. . . ."

"No," I cried.

"Shhhh, baby, it's okay. You too excited to know you come."

When I came to myself and realized what I'd done I turned
away from her.

"That's okay," she whispered, rubbing my butt with her
palm. "You already loved me enough, baby. Sleep now." She
was quivering against my back as I fell asleep.

MOUSE AND I WERE STANDING in the swamp and mosquitoes were all over me. My crotch was the worst bit, and I
scratched until it was raw. Mouse told me that I was going to
scratch it right off, then he started laughing.

"If you stop scratchin'," he said, "they stop bitin' you, fool!"

The wind was blowing in a loud rush all around. I turned to

see Momma Jo making the wind with her breathing. She came
up to me like a big cloud, and made like to kiss me but instead
she breathed down my throat. It was a powerful smell but I
couldn't pull away from her—she was too strong.

I was pushed to the ground. She was so heavy that I could
hear my bones snap, one at a time. At every crack Ernestine
moaned.

Momma came up with my butcher's knife. I knew she was
going to cut off my head to make her young again. I wanted to
yell for Mouse to come save me but I couldn't catch my wind
without her breath in me.

WE WERE ALL at the dinner table. Daddy and my mother and
two little girls that I had never seen. A big gray stallion was
heaped on the table. It had been roasted with potatoes and
carrots, and it smelled like Momma Jo's pussy. My mother
(who was a big woman) stood up and came toward me. All I
could see was yards and yards of her gray plaid dress coming at
me like a freighter coming into the Gulf.

"EASY! EASY!" Mouse was whispering in my ear. "Wake up,
man! We gotta go! Com'on!"

I was sick in my heart. I moaned out loud, and Mouse said,
"Shut up. You gonna wake'er."

Mouse pulled me by the arm but I was too weak to move. I
could see that he was wearing a long gray coat.

"Lemme 'lone," I said.

"Easy, this ain't no time t'play."

"Raymond?" Her voice came from somewhere in the dark
room. "Raymond, that you?"

"Yeah, Jo. I come t'collect Easy."

"What time is it?"

"It's still dark."

"When you be back?"

"I dunno. In a few days, or less."

"What you need Easy for?" She said it like a challenge.

"He my friend, Jo, like I tole you."

"Well. You go on out an' I sen'im in a minute."

Mouse leaned close to me and smiled his golden smile. He winked, then he was gone out the door.

A match struck and Momma Jo was there lighting an oil lantern. Shadows jumped around the room and I wondered if it was really night outside. She was just as tall but she looked different when she was naked. Her breasts made her look more human, they didn't stick straight out anymore but they didn't sag very much either. The hard nipples curved upward like blunted black barbs on a thornbush.

"Mo'nin', Easy," she said gently. "How you?"

There was a moan and the rustling of blankets and I could see Ernestine lying on the pillows from where Momma Jo came; Clifton was nowhere to be seen.

Momma tossed a blanket over the girl and wrapped another one around her own shoulders. She asked me to sit down there on the floor, but I shook my head and picked up my pants.

She stood close to me while I dressed, letting her shoulders sag down so she was close to my height. "You gonna come back wit' Raymond, baby?"

"No, I don't think so."

"Why not?"

"Well, I gotta job you know, an' we jes' gonna say hi to his fam'ly, then we gone."

"Raymond say he comin' back."

"I ain't got the time." I looked her in the face for a second. Her eyes were full of sympathy or pity; I didn't know what for.

"You had some time las' night."

There was nothing to say to that so I concentrated on the buttons of my shirt.

"Why'ont you come back t'say bye?"

"Okay." I lied to keep her quiet, but she looked down at Ernestine and then back at me.

"You shouldn't be mad 'bout us girls gettin' together, Easy. She just excited an' you an' Clifton was out. Girls need t'talk 'bout they men." She smiled and looked coy.

I wanted to tear off my skin.

"I don't care 'bout them. I gotta go an' I'll come say bye fo' we get back down."

I moved to go to the door, but she touched my arm.

"Come back, Easy," she said, and I felt something.

"I cain't, Jo. This ain't right, an', an' you don't even know me."

She looked at me for a long time. While she did she seemed to get older and older; her eyes were tired and there were folds in her face. It was like she was aging to death and I was killing her. The lantern was fluttering, maybe it had been the whole time, but right then I thought that if the light went out she'd die.

"Okay," I said. "But just to say bye."

When she kissed me I felt sick but excited too; I wanted to scream.

When I got to the door she said, "You watch out fo'
Raymond, honey."

"Mouse don't need me t'help him."

"I mean you make sure you don't get hurt. Raymond hate
this place an' he don't have no good reason t'be down here."

"I be okay, Jo."

She put her hand on my throat like she was going to choke
me, but softly.

Then I left.

5

THE SKY WAS BLACK and crowded with stars. The land was like a heaven too; everywhere there were clusters of fireflies, glowing white with glints of green and yellow and blue. They covered the ground in a shimmering net of light. In the middle of that light was the dark form of a man holding a yellow lantern.

"Hey, Easy! She let you go, huh?"

"Where'd you go?" I asked Mouse. "How come you left me there?"

"I had t'go see my friend, Easy. I figgered you could take care'a yo'self." Mouse snickered. "Who gonna figger you for runnin' after witch pussy?"

I took two steps toward him with my fists clenched.

"Hole'it, man." He was laughing and holding the lantern out as a play shield. "If Momma go after somebody, then what can they do? We just people, Easy, and she is more'n that."

"What you go'n leave me for?"

"I had t'see somebody. I din't know what's on that crazy woman's mind."

"Shit!"

Mouse was laughing so hard that he had trouble holding the lantern steady; his whole body shook.

"Easy, you shoulda been born rich," he said, letting out a long sigh of pleasure. "I mean up on the hill with servants and tea."

"What you talkin' 'bout?"

"Look at you. Here you go wantin' t'pick'n choose like you too good fo'Jo. But you don't un'erstan'—that's Momma Jo in there. If she like you then you halfway got it made. She feed you and fix you up if you get cut. Shit! An' I bet she fuck you bettah than all them chippies you be chasin' in Houston. I tell ya. You got a woman wanna take you home you better not be turnin' up yo' nose . . ."

"Shut up, shut up!"

"All right." He hunched his shoulders. "All I gotta say is . . ."

"Just shut up, all right?"

And he did. He turned and walked away without another word. I followed him, my head about to come open with all that had happened.

With those stars and lightning bugs I barely made out the path we walked on from the heavens. It was like walking in the black skies of night; my whole sense of up and down was gone. The only thing that kept me from getting dizzy was keeping my eye on Mouse's black silhouette, rushing on up ahead. We walked for quite a while until we came into a stand of cypress trees.

"This it," he said.

"This is what?"

"This is where we gonna meet'im."

"Meet who?"

"Now you gotta make up yo' mind, Easy."

"What you say?"

"Well, either you want me t'talk or you don't."

"I don't want you talkin' 'bout that woman or nuthin' t'do wit' what happened back there."

He shook his head, saying, "I cain't go along with that. When I talks, I talks an' that's it. If you don't wanna hear me then I shet my mouf. But if you wanna hear, then you gotta take whatever come inta my head, 'cause that's the way I am. I cain't be bothered wit' you wanna be hearin' one thing but you don' wanna be hearin' nuthin' else. . . ."

He went on like that, running his mouth. The drift of his palaver was that he couldn't afford to hold back anything because it might be something important and he'd never know unless he got it out.

"I think wit' my mouf, Easy. I might say sumpin' that sounds like shit t'you, but once I say it then I know sumpin' else 'bout what I be needin t'do."

I could see that he was excited and that he needed to talk, so I let him go on; as long as he didn't bring up Jo I was happy to let him rave.

After he ran out of things to say we just sat there. I could see a little better by then because morning nosed at the horizon.

"What's standin' out here in the middle'a the night gonna do 'bout yo' weddin'?" I asked, wanting to break the silence.

"Sh!"

There came the sound of rustling branches.

"Ray?" a man called out.

"Over here, Brother Dom," Mouse cooed.

Out from the trees came something. I knew it was a man because I heard him call to us but it could have been something else. He leaned way over to the side, one arm hanging down almost to the ground. He walked in a shuffle that made his whole body twist like a silkworm hanging from her thread. His back was hunched over so his head looked like it sprouted from the chest. His mouth was open wide with misshapen teeth grown in all directions; the giant maw glistened.

"Hey, brother," Mouse said, then he did something I'd never seen him do with a man before—he hugged the hunchback. A real hug with their cheeks touching.

"This here is Easy, the one I tole you 'bout," Mouse said. "Easy, I want you t'shake hands with my oldest friend, Domaque."

The hunchback swung his long arm at me and it was all I could do not to jump back. His hand was leathery, dry, and strong.

"Easy!" he said like I was old and deaf. "My brother tole me 'bout you. Glad t'meetcha."

"Yeah," I said. "Sure."

"This here's Jo's boy, Easy. Easy stayed wit' yo momma last night, Dom."

"Uh-huh. Wanna go fishin' now?"

As it got lighter I could see that one of Domaque Jr.'s eyes was dead; it was brown and receded into the socket.

"Sure, I got my rod here in my pocket." Mouse slapped his pants. "But you got what I want?"

Domaque ducked his head even lower, I couldn't tell if he was ashamed or happy.

He said, "Yeah, I got it out to the house."

Mouse smiled. "Well then, com'on. Let's get us some fish!"

Domaque screamed and jumped and hurried away; Mouse went after him, and I followed Mouse.

"I tole ya I'ma show you how t'fish, Easy."

"You ain't even got no fishin' pole," I said.

"Ohhhhh, but I do."

"YEAH, EASY." Mouse leaned back against an old elm looking out into Rags Pond. It was a largish body of water with a thin mist clinging to its sleek surface. "Me an' Dom go way back. Huh, Dom?"

Domaque ducked his head and chortled. "That's right, brother. We been friends since we was little."

"God's truth, Ease." Mouse held up a hand in a swearing motion. "Me an' Dom went through it when we was kids. You know they picked on me 'cause I was so little, an' they pestered Dom cause'a his hump. But you know wit' my mind an' Dom's size we roughed up they little butts."

The morning was darker than it was light but day was coming on fast. Live oaks completely surrounded the pond. The oaks had gray moss hanging from them into the water. Mouse reached under his coat, into the back of his pants, and came out with a long-barreled .41-caliber pistol. He smiled. Domaque howled and waved his fists in circles.

"Shhhh." Mouse waved at him.

Dom put both hands to his mouth.

"You know we cain't be yellin'," Mouse said. "It's time. Easy, you an' Dom go sit on the rocks an' keep quiet. You got that sack right, bro?"

"Yeah, Ray. I got it," Dom said.

"All right then! Let's get us food fo' the wintah!"

Mouse rolled up his cuffs to just below the knee. I couldn't figure out why he did that, because then he waded into the water up to his waist. In one hand he had the pistol and in the other he had some crackers or dry bread that he pulled from his shirt pocket. He sprinkled the crumbs on the water and stood stock still.

Behind Mouse stood the half-circle of twenty-odd live oaks. A jury of old men with gray moss beards. Over them was the glimmer of a weak yellow sun in a sky that just hinted blue. There was no breeze or sound at all. Mouse looked like a big man, bigger than life, out in that water. He was taller than the trees, and the only thing that stood out from the pond.

"In the beginnin' God made the heavens an' the lands," Domaque said from behind me. "An' there was darkness in the land and the face of God was on the water . . ."

Dom went on and on whispering with his version of Genesis.

Out in the water, just to the left of where Mouse stood, came a sucking sound and a droplet of water leaped up into the air. Then to the right, two droplets, also with sucking sounds.

"And God went beyond the waters and he called that heaven . . ." Domaque said while dozens of droplets plopped into the water. It was the sound of rain under a clear sky.

Mouse slowly scattered the last of his bread into the pond. Then, carefully and slowly, like a stalking cat raising his claws, Mouse brought the pistol over his head, holding it with both hands so that the barrel pointed at the water; his thumbs were on the trigger and his fingers were laced around the butt.

When he fired, dozens of mallards and pelicans started from behind the oaks. Dom Jr. let out a yell that started at a low warble and peaked at a siren's whine.

Mouse yelled, "Com'on, Dom! Get yo' sack out here fo' they get away!"

Dom looped the sack around his neck with a rope that was stitched around the lip of the bag. He splashed in, bouncing up and down in the water like a very small child at the shore.

"Com'on, Ease!" Mouse called. "We need some help wit' all'a these here!"

He kept on shouting while I got off my shoes and socks and put them on my sitting rock. By the time I waded out to them they had turned away, catching fish with their hands and shoving them into the large burlap sack. When I was up to my hips in water I saw the unconscious fish. It seemed like hundreds of them but I guess it couldn't have been so many. Pale white underbellies of gar, catfish, carp, and other fish I had never seen. They shuddered in the water like they were dead. Mouse told me later that it was the force of the hollow-nosed soft-lead bullet hitting the water that knocked them out.

"That's why you gotta catch'em quick," he said. "Fo' they come awake an' slip down 'tween yo' legs."

It was terrible.

Mouse lunged one-handed, because he had his pistol held high in the other hand, going for fish after fish. Dom was yucking and yelling. He was clumsy and barely got as many with two hands as Mouse did with one. I didn't grab any. It was like a bad dream to see all those fish quivering and half dead. I don't mind catching a fish or wringing a hen's neck, but that slaughter left me sick.

ON THE LAST DAY I saw my father, he took me down to the slaughterhouse. It was an awful place. They had cows walking down an aisle that came to a sharp turn. When the cow took the turn she came to a window and a big man hit her on top of the head with a sledgehammer; she'd hit the floor shaking just like those fish. From there a conveyor belt took the body to a man with a curved sword. He caught a mean-looking hook in her carcass and then had his helpers lift her up off of the ground. Then he cut her jugular. At first the hot blood sprayed out; then it slowed to a pumping ooze. When the bleeding had almost stopped he cut her open from crotch to throat. The blood flowed down the sides of the killing floor into gutters underneath the room. The blood and the leavings down there were what made the room smell rotten. The smell of death by the dozens and by the hundreds; death so strong that my eyes burned and I gagged, but I wouldn't let myself throw up because I was afraid to vomit in blood.

The foreman was a white man with great big arms and blood all down his thick apron. His curved knife was black and pitted, but you could see it was sharp by the way it cut through the cow's shoulder joint; it made a tearing sound as it reaped. He was taller than anyone else in the slaughterhouse.

My father stood up straight and said, "You said it was seventeen dollars an' this here is only 'bout half that."

"I ain't got time t'talk to you, boy. You take what you can git."

My father stood up taller as if he was trying to get to be as tall as that white man; I got behind him and grabbed onto his pants.

"You made me a deal, Mr. Mischew, and I want what's mines."

"Niggah?" the white man exclaimed as he slapped the flat of the blade on his apron. "You want sumpin? 'Cause you know I'm just the man give it to ya."

If that white man did much business with my father he must've known that he was always soft-spoken and respectful. But when you cheat a man and call him nigger—and his boy is standing there too? Well that was why Mr. Mischew looked so surprised when he found himself flat on his back on the bloody floor.

MOUSE CUT OPEN A FISH and handed the limp corpse over to Dom, who scooped out the entrails and rinsed it in the pond.

I was sick and ashamed of being sick. My head felt hot.

"Hey, Easy. You don't look too good, son." Mouse smiled gently. "Why'ont you take a little nap. We get ya when it's time t'go t'Dom's."

"What you need all them fish fo', man? We cain't eat all that."

"Put 'em in the smoker," Domaque said. "Smoke 'em up an' we got fish all the time. Go down t'Miss Alexander an' trade some fo'drinks in the bar." Then he laughed and Mouse laughed and they kept on pulling guts out and tossing them into the water.

"I'ma go back on t'Houston," I said. "I ain't got no mo' time fo'this mess."

"Com'on, Easy, gimme a break." Mouse's mouth made a smile but his eyes were deadly. "Dom got a weddin' gift fo'me but he wanna go fishin' first. I tole you in the car we gonna go fishin'.'"

"How much longer you wanna be down here?"

"Just a couple'a mo' days. Anyway I need ya t'go out t'my stepdaddy's wit' me."

"Why?"

Mouse pointed a limp gar at me. "That man is the devil, Ease. Ain't no way I can go out there alone."

"Com'on, Raymond, I ain't never known you t'be scared'a nothin'."

"I am afraid of him," he said.

"Abraham had cattle and silver and gold," Dom was saying as he led us through deep thickets toward his house. "An' Lot was wit' him an' so was Abraham's wife."

"What you always sayin', Dom?" I asked.

"Rememberin' the Bible like Miss Dixon say."

"What's that?"

"She say that to know the word you gotta make the Bible yo' own. You gotta know the stories just like they happened t'friends'a yours." He laughed and went on, "An' they was so rich that they built diff'rent houses an' after a time they vied fo'the land."

Mouse came up next to me and said, "Dom wanna be a preacher, Ease. He always readin' the Bible an' whatnot. You know he's a well-learnt boy, that ole white woman Dixon make him read ev'rythang."

"Who's that?" I asked, suddenly jealous of that freak's knowledge. "How come she gonna teach him his letters?"

"Just a crazy white woman, Ease. She ain't got no knittin' so she take on charities."

We came to the clearing after an hour or so.

Dom's house was an abandoned molasses shack. It was small and dilapidated but it was also nice because he had flowers growing all around it. Sunflowers on either side and golden wild-rose bushes along the pebbled path that led to the front door. There were thick leafy bushes of pink dahlias at odd places in the yard. It looked as though all the flowering plants were wild but I knew they weren't because there were no weeds to be seen. Sweet pea vines wound up the loose timbers that shored up the east wall of the shack. Purple passion fruit flowers knotted through the ash branches that surrounded the dale. There were other flowers of white and red but I didn't know what kind they were, and neither did Dom.

Underneath the sweet peas was a clear patch of earth that was covered with the body parts of hard-rubber baby dolls. Arms and feet and heads with golden and brown hair. Mostly they were white dolls like the well-to-do white children have but there were some colored ones too. It looked like a pile of infant corpses washed up from their tiny graves in a terrible storm.

"You got chirren, Dom?" I asked.

He gave a high squeal that might have been pleasure and said, "Them there is my chirren, Easy." Then he chuckled and Mouse did too.

Dom said that his "room" was too small for all us guests,

so he went in and came out with three crates for us to sit on. It was very pleasant to sit out there in his wild yard. A garden as beautiful as any I'd seen in the rich part of Houston; it was almost like an inside room or greenhouse only with the sky for a roof. I told Dom how much I liked it and he smiled.

"I'm always doin' sumpin' t'make it bettah," he said. "I'ma start puttin' in fruit trees next year an' by the time they grows maybe I have me a wife t'share 'em wit'." He looked out over his garden with that terrible smile and dead eye.

"Well, Dom, we got yo' fish, now what you got fo'me?" Mouse said in his taking-care-of-business voice.

"I got it, Ray, right in the house."

"Well let's have it. Easy an' me got some miles t'cover fo' we can rest."

There were hummingbirds at the sweet peas, flicking in and out of the blossoms so fast you could hardly tell they were there. I felt funny, light-headed, but I didn't want it to change. It seemed to me that this was the Eden Dom talked about; like he built his own garden right out of the Bible.

"Here you go, Ray." Dom handed Mouse a doll that had been burned and mutilated. It had once been a white baby doll but the hard-rubber skin was now burnt black and the clothes it wore were the overalls that a farmer wore. The brown hair was clipped short and the arms were straight out as if it were being crucified on an invisible cross. The eyes were painted over as the wide white eyes you see on a man when he's frightened and trying to see everything coming his way.

Mouse smiled and took the doll from Dom. It seemed that

Dom was a little uneasy about giving away his ugly toy but I knew that it was hard saying no to Mouse.

"Thank you, brother," Mouse said. "Daddy Reese gonna just love it."

Mouse's laugh filled Dom's garden until all the flowers seemed to vibrate with it.

6

WHAT'S THAT DOLL FO'?" I asked Mouse.
We'd been walking for miles. He was moody again,
the way he'd been when he and Etta first got engaged.

"Just sumpin', man. Nuthin'."

"You went th'ough all that fo'nuthin'?"

"It's sumpin', I tole ya!"

It was a quiet country path, far enough away from water to
be light on insects but close enough to have trees and wildlife.
I was coming down with something. My hands were cold and
the inside of my head felt like cotton wadding.

"How come Domaque make them dolls?" I asked.

At first I thought he was going to ignore me, but after a few
steps he said, "Dom started makin' 'em when we was small. Ya
see, Dom got a crazy mad temper. He ain't slow or nuthin,'
'cause you know he can read as good as that white woman
teach'im. But he got nerves. Somebody make fun'a him an' he

start to shake an' the next thing you know he's actin' crazy. When we was little the other kids would mess wit' us, 'specially when we all get together after Sunday school. One time this little boy, Bunny Drinkwater, started to rag po' ole Dom till Dom was a tremblin' leaf. An' that just made all the other kids join in laughin'. But they didn't know that Dom had carried a butcherin' knife wit'im that day. He never said why but I guess he was tired'a bein' the fool. Anyway he took out after Bunny but Bunny was quick an' Dom couldn't move fast t'save his life so we all was expectin' Dom t'throw that knife down an' cry. . . . But that's not what happened."

A red fox ran out into the road ahead of us. It looked up at Mouse and pulled its head back like it recognized Raymond. Then it turned tail and slipped off into the brush. Mouse laughed and seemed to get into a better mood.

"Anyway . . . Dom went out after Bunny swinging his knife so wild that I half expected he was gonna cut his own self; but then Bunny tripped. All the little boys screamed like girls. Dom swung down t'gut little Bunny but he missed and just kinda cut him on the arm. Bunny was so scared by that little cut that he was frozen on the ground an' Dom raised his hand fo' the kill. . . ." Mouse stared off into the woods, remembering something. I was afraid to hear the rest. "Shit. One'a the big boys runned out and grabbed Dom fo' he could finish it. You know I always feel bad when I think'a that; like I'm missin' sumpin'."

"But what 'bout the dolls?"

"Yeah." Mouse picked up a thick branch from the path and started snicking off the switches to smooth it into a pole. "I tole Dom that he had t'git hold'a hisself 'cause the folks 'round there didn't like humpbacks killin' they babies. That's when he got his first doll. He dressed it up like Bunny. He tore at it and pissed on it; threw it in a sty an' let the pigs stamp it." Mouse laughed to himself. "Yeah, Easy, he had a fine ole time wit' his dolls. An' only me an' Jo knew it."

AFTER A WHILE the path grew crooked and rutty. The branches hung so low that I had to walk stooped over half of the time. Mouse said that the road had once been the way to town from his stepfather's farm but that Reese let it go to seed years before, after Mouse's natural mother died.

"The ole man fell apart after Momma died," Mouse said.

When we got close enough to see the place Mouse stopped, wiped his mouth, and stared.

I was feeling tired so I said, "Well, let's git on wit' it. That's it, right?"

Mouse didn't say a word.

"Raymond." I hoped his real name would shock him into moving.

"Yeah?"

"Let's go."

"Uh-huh," he said, but he didn't move.

"What we waitin' fo'?"

His eyes were colder than all winter long.

"I'm scared, Easy."

"We cain't turn back."

"Why not?" he asked like a child might.

"What kinda fool you gonna feel like if you come all the way out here an' then you don't even ask? You cain't tell, you know, he might reach in his pocket an' come out wit' the bread."

That seemed to tickle Mouse. The winter passed and he smiled.

"All right, Easy. We see what he got t'give."

THE YARD, if you could call it that, was a mess. There was an old wagon that had both of its axles broken, the rusted-out metal hulk of a steam boiler, and pointy-spouted oil cans scattered around. There was a jumbled pile of old bales of hay that must've laid there for five years and more. Old furniture tossed anywhere and many things I couldn't even put a name to. I got the feeling that the old farmer went into a rage, taking everything he had and throwing it from the house and barn.

Little animals scurried in amongst the junk; there were mounds of ants; an opossum had made its nest in a hollow tree full of old clothes, rags.

There was a large stack of rotting timber that must've been intended for building at one time, lying in front of the house like a giant pile of dropped kindling.

A few wild roosters hopped around and four mongrel dogs sat in the shade of a sweet olive tree. The ground around them was scattered with dried turds and dead blades of grass.

The house was even worse.

It looked as if the main beams had been broken. The roof was caved in; all four walls leaned inward. The old two-story farmhouse had been folded into a squat hut. There was a pipe sticking out near the top of one of the slanted walls, a weak rag of smoke coming from it. If it wasn't for that I'd've thought we had come on a deserted wreck.

One of the dogs got up, snarling and slavering at Mouse. It snapped and growled but just when it got near, Mouse slammed it on the side of the neck with his pole. It was a very simple thing; he did it almost like breathing, he was so blasé.

The dog's yelp was so sharp that you could feel his pain. He rolled in the filth under the tree, making a terrible racket. The other dogs jumped up and started pacing, back and forth.

That's when some boards that were once the front door of the house moved outward. A strong-looking black man stood in the wreck of that doorway. He wore overalls with no shirt and you could see the strength in his arms and chest like flats of dark steel. He looked like he belonged in the fields all day long, tearing up the sod and yanking trees out by the root.

Mouse dropped his stick. "Hey there, Reese," he said.

The big man came out of the doorway but he seemed to bring the shadows along with him.

"This here's my friend—Easy Rawlins."

I said hello but the farmer didn't even look at me. He was watching his dog, who by then had stopped wallowing and was simply lying in the dirt, shivering like one of the fish Mouse had stunned earlier that morning.

"Wha' happen my dog, Raymond?"

"Search me. He run up like he knew me an' then he fell into a fit." Mouse stared Reese straight in the face. He wasn't letting anything show, except a slight squint from the sun.

"Ain't no room in the house fo'no guests, Ray. What you want?"

Mouse hunkered down against a rotted bale of hay and said, "Just wanted to shout at ya, Reese. You know it's been some years an' I thought I'd see ya while we down here."

"I ain't got no food and no drinks fo' guests neither. So if you got sumpin' t'say then let's have it."

I was sorry I talked Mouse into coming.

"Looks like you could use a hand out here, Reese. Farm's goin' to shit if you ask me."

Reese took a deep breath, you could see the rage. Watching Mouse bait him was like watching a man striking matches over a vat of gasoline.

"I mean you might need some help out here an', well you know I'm kinda settlin' down nowadays . . . gettin' married to a girl down in Houston."

Reese was through with small talk.

"So I thought maybe we talk some business. You know after my weddin' I might wanna come on out here an' do some honest work."

That got a smile from Reese. He said, "No, uh-uh. You go on an' do whatever it is you doin'. I stay out to here."

"Well we don't have to worry 'bout that now. I thought you wanna come on out an' celebrate wit' me an' Easy. You know it ain't ev'ryday you get a daughter-in-law an' maybe some grandkids."

"I gotta take care'a my dog . . ." Reese said. He turned to go back into the house.

"Reese!" Mouse shouted as he jumped to his feet.

The older man stopped. Without turning he said, "I don't take to folks raisin' they voice t'me out on my farm, an' I don't take t'folks comin' out an' hurtin' my dogs. So I guess you better go back to wherever you come from or I'ma go get my gun an' . . ."

"I come fo'my part'a Momma's dowry, Reese," Mouse said. "I know she had some jewelry an' some money from her folks when you two got married an' you leased land wit' it. I know

you got money out here now, an' I want some for my own weddin'. It's mines, Reese, an' I want it."

The last three words turned Reese around.

I fell back a step while he and Mouse faced off.

"You ain't got the right t'say her name, boy. She up ev'ry night
worried 'bout you an' who knows what you doin', or where? She
worried herself sick an' then she died an' who you think brought
it on?" There were tears in Reese's eyes. "She died askin' fo'you.
It broke my heart, an' where was you? You weren't nowhere.
Nowhere. An' my girl layin' in that bed all yellah an' sick 'cause
she so worried 'bout a rotten chile like you . . ."

"What good it gonna do, huh?" Mouse shouted. "I's barely
a teenager an' you come after me wit' sticks an' fists. What
good it gonna do her t'see you beat me?"

"You was a rotten boy, Raymond, an' you's a rotten man.
You kilt her an' now you want my money, but I see you dead
fo' I give up a dime."

"I kilt'er? You the one. You the one ravin' 'bout how yo' boy
so good an' how I ain't even legal. You the one beat on her an'
beat on me which hurt her even more 'cause my momma was
a good woman an' you is the devil! The devil, you hear?"
Mouse reached into the back of his pants for the second time
that day. He pulled out that long-barreled .41 and blasted that
poor shivering dog. Then he shot the other three: crack, crack,
crack; like ducks in an arcade. Reese hit the ground thinking
that Mouse was gunning for him.

"I'ma have what's mines," Mouse said as he brought the
bead down on Reese.

"You can kill me an' you can take my soul but I ain't gonna
give you a drop'a what's mine!"

"Raymond!" I shouted. "Let it go, man! You cain't get nuthin' like this. Let it go."

Mouse lifted the barrel a hair and shot over Reese's head, then he turned to me and said, "We better get outta here."

We went fast down the way we had come.

Half a mile down, Mouse stopped and pulled the baby doll from his jacket. He took out a string and tied it roughly around the doll's neck and then he hung the doll from a branch so that it dangled down over the center of the road.

"He gonna come down here with that shotgun but you know he gonna be stopped by this," Mouse said loudly, to himself.

WE TOOK SO MANY TURNS and shortcuts that I was lost. I think Mouse was lost too, because when it started getting dark he said, "We cain't get nowhere's good t'night, Ease. We better find some shelter."

Nothing could've sounded worse to me. When we were running I'd started coughing and it wouldn't go away. I was feverish and dizzy and I wanted my bed and my room in Houston more than anything.

"Ain't they noplace?"

"Uh-uh, Ease. Anyway, I want to go to ground. Reese is good at night."

He left me to rest next to a dead oak and went out looking for shelter. While I sat there, beginning to fade into my fever, I saw a barn owl glide through the low branches. It moved fast and silent and it never hit a twig, it was so sure. I thought to myself that some rabbit was going to die that night, then I started to shake; whether it was from the fear of mortality or chills I didn't know.

"There's a lea some hunter musta used just a ways down, Ease," Mouse said when he returned.

"What if Reese use it?"

"He ain't likely to be in no lea t'night. If he go out huntin' it'a be wide awake."

We lay side by side in that flat tent of leaves and baling wire. The grippe came full on me.

"Wh-what you kill them dogs fo'?"

Raymond put his arm around me and held on tight to keep me from shivering. He said, "Shhh, Easy, you sick. Git some sleep and in the mo'nin' you be fine."

"I-I-I just wanna know why. Why you kill them dogs?"

I felt like a cranky baby half napping on a Sunday afternoon.

"I was mad, that's all, Ease," Mouse whispered. "Reese talk 'bout my momma like that an' I'm like to kill'im."

"But them dogs didn't hurt you."

"Go t'sleep now, Easy. Shh."

I never knew Mouse to be so gentle. He held me all night and kept me warm as much as he could. Who knows? Maybe I would've died out there in Pariah if Mouse hadn't held me to his black heart.

7

WHEN I WOKE UP things seemed better. Dew weighed heavily on the grass and leaves around us. It was bright and early. A jay stood not five feet from us with a grasshopper crumpled in its beak. The jay looked at me and for some reason that made me happy.

I could smell Mouse's sour breath from over my shoulder; there was a tiny wheeze coming from him. Dead dogs and crazy family were far away for the moment. I felt a cough coming on but I stifled it to stay quiet just a little longer.

"You 'wake, Easy?"

"Yeah."

"How you feel?"

I tried to say "fine" but that started me coughing.

When I finally stopped Mouse crawled out of the lea and said, "We better get you someplace inside so you can rest. We better git you back t'Jo's."

"Uh-uh. I ain't goin' there."

"Jo ain't gonna do nuthin' when you sick, Easy. And she's the closest thing to a doctor for twenty miles."

"I ain't goin' t'Jo's. No!"

"You cain't be comin' wit' me, Ease. Reese come up 'hind me an' I gotta move, fast."

"Why'ont we go on home?"

"I ain't finished yet. I made up my mind I'ma git what's mines outta that man an' that's what I'ma do."

"He tole you no."

"That's all right. I ain't hesitatin' yet. We got some more ground t'cover—me an' Daddy Reese."

"I ain't goin' t'Jo's."

"Okay. I take you over to Miss Dixon's. She always willin' t'he'p if she think you know Dom."

"Who is she?" I asked, not trusting Mouse too much anymore.

He laughed a good laugh and said, "Don't worry, Easy, she too old t'be thinkin' 'bout love. Anyway, she's white."

IT WAS A BEAUTIFUL DAY.

We made it down to some railroad tracks and followed them for a few miles. It was one of those sultry Southern mornings when all of the sounds of birds and insects are muffled by the heavy air. I was so weak that I couldn't bring myself to worry about what Mouse was planning; all I wanted was a bed somewhere and some food.

After almost an hour we came to a large field that abutted a smooth dirt road. Across the road was a house. It was a real house with a garden and a fence and all the walls standing straight.

"That's Miss Dixon's place," Mouse said. "Now you let me do the talkin', all right?"

"Uh-huh. But I ain't gonna stay there if I don't like it."

"Don't you worry, even a white man'd like this."

There was a swing chair out front. The porch was closed by a lattice covered with forsythia. When we walked up the front stairs Mouse took the lead, but before he could knock on the screen door the inner door opened.

"Raymond Alexander." It was a statement. "What you want here?"

Mouse doffed a make-believe hat and said, "Miss Dixon, I come out here on a piece of business for Domaque."

"I didn't know you were back in Pariah, Raymond. Why is that?"

Whether she was asking why she wasn't told about Raymond's return or she just wanted to know why he had come back I couldn't tell, but Mouse didn't even try to figure it out.

"Dom axed me t'ax you t'keep Easy here for a night 'cause Easy's sick. Come on up here, Ease, an' let Miss Dixon see ya."

I moved up to his side, looking as hard at that little old woman as she was at me.

"Anyway," Mouse continued, "Dom has got business down in Jenkins an' he wanted Easy someplace where he'd be warm. You know he's got the grippe an' that can come to pneumonia in a second."

"Don't I know it," she said.

"Dom said that he gonna come get Easy tomorrah if he can please stay in some ole corner t'night."

"Domaque asked you this?"

"Yes, ma'am."

"And how am I to know that Domaque asked you this?"

"Well, you know ma'am, that Dom an' me is the best of friends . . ."

"I know," she interrupted, "that you are a sinner, Raymond Alexander, and a bad influence on the ground you trod. I was hoping that you were gone forever and that that sweet poor chile Domaque was free of your evil ways."

"I'm just visitin', ma'am."

She looked at him and then at me. "Why, this boy could be as bad as you. How'm I to know?"

She moved to close the door but Mouse spoke up again. "Ma'am, I'm not lyin' to ya. Dom wants Easy t'stay wichyou 'cause Easy got the grippe, an' if you don't believe me then you feel his head an' see if I'm lyin'."

She looked suspicious for a minute but then she pushed open the screen door and came toward me. I moved back a half step, out of reflex I guess, but Mouse grabbed me and made me stand still.

Miss Dixon was a small white woman with pale hair that was pulled straight back against her head. She wore a floor-length flat green dress that had long sleeves and a neckline at the throat. She was very thin but not brittle-looking like many old white women; she could've been made from solid bone from the way her hard hand felt against my forehead.

"Lord, he's burnin' up!"

"I tole you," Mouse said.

"You a friend to Domaque, son?" she asked me.

The porch beams started shaking gently before my eyes, like leaves on a breeze.

"Yes, ma'am," I said.

"Dom come over by noon, ma'am," Mouse said. He already had a foot down the stairs.

"You tell him to bring Mr. Dickens's book, Raymond," she said to him. Then to me, "Come on inside."

I turned to say something to Mouse, but he was going down the stairs with his back to me. He was whistling and moving fast. I almost called to him but then a feeling came over me: I wanted Mouse to be far away and I didn't care what happened to him or his family; I didn't care about weddings or a good time anymore. I just wanted to sleep.

"What's your full name, son?"

"Ezekiel Rawlins, ma'am."

"Well come on in 'fore you burn a hole in my porch."

The entrance to her house had three coatracks, six umbrella stands, and more mirrors and knickknacks on the wall than I could count. There was a darkwood chair of a different make against each wall and on either side of the door. It was a small entrance room and so crowded with furniture that we two could barely fit in it at the same time.

She led me quickly through to the parlor.

This was a large room with blue velvet wallpaper from the ivory-carpeted floor to the cream-colored ceiling. There was a blue sofa, with a matching chair, and a red love seat with two matching chairs. There was a yellow couch and a brown one too. Each of them had matching chairs. The sofas and chairs were so close together that you couldn't sit on them.

There were the coffee tables: maple, cherry, pine, and mahogany; all of them stacked with every different kind of tea setting and little china sculpture that you can imagine. She had bureaus and cabinets, one behind the other; some of them had glass doors and you could make out the piles of plates and stacks of teacups.

I looked at that old woman again—she must've been in her late seventies.

I'd seen it happen before. The oldest member of the family outlives all of her husbands and siblings, and even her children sometimes, and all the belongings of all the families come to her in a big lonely house. She lives with five houses' worth of furniture and dishes, old clothes, and knickknacks.

"Come on, Ezekiel, you're in my charge now."

The next room was the music room. There were three upright pianos and different leather bags in the shapes of guitars, fiddles, and even a tuba.

"Go on, take your clothes off and get in that tub." She opened a door that led to a small washroom. I hesitated for a minute but she just shook her hand back and forth to show how impatient she was and I went in.

"You're lucky I take my bath on Wednesdays; I just filled the tub," she said, leaving me to my toilet. "And I have clothes from my uncle you can wear, he was 'bout your size."

The washroom smelled of soap. There was a brass sink and a commode and a large washtub on lion feet. Next to the sink was a table with a giant clamshell on it. The clamshell was filled with hundreds of little flowers made from soap. Red, green, and yellow soap, and violet and blue too. Each one hinted of a different spice but mostly they smelled like soap.

I took off my clothes and realized how bad I smelled after

the last two days. I tried to pile them in a corner where the smell wouldn't be too offensive in that sweet-smelling room, and then I jumped into the tub.

"Ow! Oh!" The water was so hot that I nearly jumped up. I thought she was trying to kill me.

"Nice an' hot, huh, Ezekiel? Secret to a long life is a hot bath twice a week and no liquor," she called through the closed door.

I got used to the water after a bit. The heat along with fever made me even more light-headed and tired. The sun was shining in through the lace curtains on the window. Miss Dixon— I found out later that Abigail was her first name—turned on a radio somewhere in the house and it was playing big-band music. The house was filled with the sound of scratchy clarinets and pianos. That was the finest living that I had ever experienced up to that time.

I'd wake up now and then and look at how my fingers and toes wrinkled in the water. Finally the water turned cold and I started shivering. So I got out and put on the green suit Miss Dixon had hung outside the door.

"Welllll . . . don't we look so much better," she said when I came into the kitchen. "Clean and scrubbed is halfway back to health."

"Yes, ma'am."

"You hungry, Ezekiel?"

"Yes, ma'am."

"Well you just sit down and I'll give you some stew."

There was already a plate on one of the three tables she had in the dinette. I went to a chair next to that setting but she yelled, "Not there! Sit at one of the other tables."

I didn't know what she meant but I went to the pine table near the back door and sat down.

"You know I cain't sit at the same table with you, Ezekiel," she said as she put a bowl of beef stew in front of me. "You know it's not proper for white and colored to sit together. I mean, it'd be as much an insult to your people as mine if we were to forget our place."

I watched her go to her separate seat and I thought to myself that she was crazy, but I couldn't keep my mind on it because that was the first food I'd had in almost a whole day. It was good stew too. I can still remember how it tasted of black pepper and wine.

"How do you know Domaque, Ezekiel?"

"Well, uh, well, I wanted t'learn t'read bettah, an' Mouse, I mean Raymond, tole me 'bout him." I was lying but I wasn't, not really.

"Do you read?"

"A little, ma'am. I can sign my name and make the sounds of letters . . . I know that a 'p' and a 'h' together sound like a 'f.'" I thought about Domaque quoting the Bible and about my father then. My father always told me that I should learn to read. Maybe it was because I was so weak but I felt about ready to cry.

"Reading is one of the few things that separates us from the animals, Ezekiel. You'd know all about the man they named you for if you could read."

"Yes, ma'am."

"And all you have to do is to keep on reading those sounds and asking Domaque and others about how you read. Maybe you can have someone read to you. Then you read it to yourself . . ." she said, and then she drifted off into a daydream.

We finished eating and she told me to go find a couch in the parlor to sleep on and that she'd come out there later to see how I was. But first she put a brown powder in some tea and gave it to me.

"Josephine Harker makes this out to the swamps. She's a real wonder at flu powders and the like."

I was nervous about drinking any tea that Jo had a hand in making, but I took it to be polite.

After that all I remember is lying down on the yellow couch. When I opened my eyes again it was night.

Miss Dixon was standing at the open door in a long white dress, and the moon was shining in on her. There were so many chairs and tables around that it was like being in an auditorium after a big function when all the chairs and whatnot are stacked for storage.

"You still got a fever, Ezekiel," she said out of the open door. "But I'll get some more tea and all you got to do is to go back to sleep and you'll be fine."

"Thank you, ma'am, I mean fo' the sleep, I mean." I was very uncomfortable. I wasn't used to spending much time with white people and I knew that colored people are always in danger of doing the wrong thing when they have to deal with whites. It was fine in Fifth Ward down in Houston, or in little colored towns like Pariah, usually, because there weren't any white people around for the most part. The only time I had ever spent around white people was when I was working, and then how I was to act was clear because whites were always the boss. That was easy because all I ever said was "yes" and "no"; but mainly "yes."

"That's all right, Ezekiel." She turned from the door and came back to the brown chair, about three pieces of furniture away from me. The room was dark except for the moonlight. "You know I'm a good woman if they let me be."

"I'm sure you are, ma'am. You sure been good t'me."

"You think so because you're not from around here, but if you lived here you'd be like all the rest of them."

"Dom speaks mighty well on you, ma'am." I was wishing that I could be away from there. Why did she have to talk to me? One wrong word and I could be in jail or worse.

"Domaque and his momma live in the swamp, so they're different," she said.

"They sure are diff'rent but they still like you."

Miss Dixon laughed. It was a nice laugh and she almost seemed like a normal person to me.

She said, "You don't see, Ezekiel. What I mean is that Domaque and Josephine don't mind me because I don't own the bayou lands."

"Ma'am?"

"I own just about everything else. My family owned it at first. The Dixons, the MacDoughs, and the Lambert family owned all of this way back. But they married each other and they died or they moved away and I'm the only one left. Our families had sharecropping and plantations down this way for more'n a hundred years. . . . Now it's all back to the tenants. I don't even collect rent but they know that the land is mine." She looked over at the window as if all the people of Pariah were there, looking in. "They know that one day I'm going to die and some strangers are going to come down and reclaim my property."

"Why cain't they just buy the land from you?" I really wanted to know.

"The country people are poor, Ezekiel, they couldn't get the cash to buy. But even if they could—this is my land," her voice became hard, "for me and mine. I can't just hand it over to strangers."

She was quiet for a while and I didn't dare to speak.

Then she said, "I'll get you some covers and that tea."

When she'd given me the blankets and medicine she said good night and went up to bed.

I was feeling tired but better, and I could think for a while before going to sleep. I thought about that grasshopper crushed in that jay's beak and about Miss Dixon; how she was like a bird too.

A LOT OF PEOPLE might not like how I acted with that white woman. They might ask: Why didn't he get mad? or Why would Mouse be breaking his butt to get money out of a poor farmer when this rich white lady would be so much of a better target?

Mouse was just doing what came natural to him. But there's a reason I wasn't angry then, why I'm still not angry and why the people of Pariah didn't rise up and kill that woman: It's what I call the "Sacred Cow Thinking."

Miss Dixon lived alone out in a colored community that hated her because she owned everything, even the roads they walked on. But Miss Dixon, and every other white person, was, to that colored community, like the cow is to those Hindus over in India. They'd all starve to death, let their children starve, before they'd slaughter a sacred cow. Miss Dixon was our sacred cow. She had money and land and she could read and go to fine events at the governor's house. But most of all she was white and being white was like another step to heaven. . . .

Killing her would have been worse than killing our own children; killing her, or even thinking of it, would be like killing the only dream we had.

8

THE NEXT MORNING we had breakfast but I pretended to be sicker than I felt and lay back down on the yellow couch after we ate.

It was nice that she took me in but it was strange too. I felt in danger whenever she looked at me.

At noon I was saved by a knock on the door.

"Domaque Harker," Miss Dixon said through the closed screen.

"How you do, Miss Dixon?"

"Very fine, and how are you?"

"I'm fine too, ma'am."

"And your mother?"

"I ain't seen her in two, three days, ma'am, but I'm sure she's fine and would wanna know that your health is fine too."

Dom was speaking slower than he had when I was with

him. I figured that Miss Dixon was teaching him how to talk as
well as read.

"And what story are you working on now, Domaque?"

"I'm workin' on Noah's tale, ma'am."

All of this talk was still through the closed screen.

"And how does that go?"

"How Noah saw the storm comin' an' how he gathered all
the married children an' all the pairs of animals. How he rode
the storm of God's righteous anger in love of his wife and his
chirren an' their chirren . . ."

"That's the way you have to do it. Make it your own."

She opened the door with that and Domaque shambled in.
That skinny woman and barrel-shaped hunchback looked so
strange standing there amongst the umbrella stands and mirrors. To look at them you would say that they had nothing in
common. But there they were understanding each other so well
that they could have been good friends, or even blood. They
would never even sit down at the same table to break bread. But
they'd get together and tell each other stories and laugh and be
happy. I remember feeling loneliness watching them.

Miss Dixon asked us to stay to dinner but Dom said that we
had to be going, being polite I guess. She gave us some sand-
wiches and fruit in a paper bag to eat on the way.

I was hoping that she'd let me keep her uncle's suit but she
didn't. My clothes smelled all the worse for the few hours of
cleanliness that I'd been given.

She waved good-bye from the front porch like a mother
sending her kids off to school. I felt bad about leaving in some
ways. I had never stayed in such a fine house and I liked it; but
I was glad to be clear of that strange white lady.

"She funny, huh?" Domaque asked.

"Yeah, I guess. She comes right out and says what she thinks and don't care how it sounds."

Dom smiled to himself and then closed his lips over his giant mouth. When he did that his lips came together in a point as if he were trying to kiss something very small.

He said, "Yeah, that's why I like her, I guess."

"I don't know if it's too good always sayin' anything you feel."

"Yeah, but that way you don't get beholdin' t'some'un. She teach me how t'read but not so's that I owe her nuthin'. I know she do it fo'her pleasure, not mine."

Afternoon was overcast and cooler than it had been. I was feeling better but after we'd walked a few miles I was ready to rest. Dom said that Pariah was only a short ways and I had a bed waiting for me there.

"A bed where?" I asked him.

"Out at Miss Alexander's."

"She any kin to Mouse?"

"She Raymond's momma's sister."

"An' what's she like?" I didn't want to tell Dom about me and his mother, that wouldn't have been proper. But I didn't want a repeat of my one night in the woods either.

"Mouse said you might be worried 'bout stayin' there. He tole me t'tell you that you be safe wit' his auntie."

When Dom walked he put his right foot forward and reached into the air with his right hand as if he were carrying a staff; his left hip would fall back and then he'd bring the left leg up with a dragging movement, straightening his shoulders as he went. He was able to walk very fast in that odd way.

When I asked him what else it was that Mouse said, that walk became even more peculiar.

"He said . . ." Dom couldn't go on for laughing and drooling.

"What?" I was worried that Mouse had told him about Jo and me; that this grinning came just before Dom pulled out his butchering knife.

"He said . . ." Dom ducked his head. ". . . that maybe he knows a girl be my friend."

PARIAH LOOKED WILDER than the woods. It was a crooked town, not more than two blocks of unpaved red clay street— and all there was to it was the one street. The north side of town was at least eight feet higher ground than the south side. Crossing the rutted and eroded road between them was more like going up- or downhill. All the buildings were made from the same weathered wood and only one of them got to three floors.

There were no telephone wires or cars or any sign at all that we were in the modern age. If people were out in front of a building, on the raised wooden platform they had for sidewalk, and they were sitting in a chair—well, it was a homemade chair, something somebody threw together one morning before breakfast and then they sat in it for the next thirty years.

But there weren't too many people outside. A couple of women carrying large baskets on their heads and one lone buggy drawn by a spotted mare. The buggy was at such an angle on that slanted road that I expected to see it turn over at any minute. But it didn't, of course, it's only cars that need flat pavement.

All the buildings looked more or less the same. You could tell them apart though, by the signs. The church had two white crosses on the front doors and the barbershop had a red-and-white-striped candy cane painted on the wall. The general store, which was also the bar, had a wooden Indian out front.

"Here we go," Dom said when we got to the wooden Indian. "Miss Alexander's general store and music bar."

It was a country store. Canned goods along the walls and fresh food on a counter at the back. There was one rack for dresses and men's jackets and a table full of shirts, socks, and shoes. Three men were playing cards and drinking at a table in the center of the room. It was a big room and, for the most part, empty.

"Hi, Dom," one of the cardplayers said.

"Afternoon, Domaque," hailed a big woman from behind the counter.

"Miss Alexander!" Dom yelled. "This here is Easy, friend'a Raymond."

"Well . . ." She smiled and showed us a mouthful of gold-rimmed teeth. "I've heard a lot about you, baby." She smiled again, turning her profile on us. "Raymond think the sun rise and set on you."

"But he still don't come out till night," I said.

That big colorful woman let out a laugh so loud that it almost knocked me over. She was wearing a bright white dress with giant blue flowers embroidered on it, a dress like the Mexicans wear to Carnival.

"He said that you was all taciturn 'cause you was sick but he didn't say that you was funny too."

She had large eyes that followed everything happening in

the room. If somebody raised their voice at the card table she was taking it in. If someone walked in the door, her eyes said hello to them, but the whole time she was talking to me and Dom.

"Raymond say he want you t'stay wit' us a couple'a days," she said. "I got a room right out back that you can use, an' on weekends we got entertainment. I mean we ain't got nuthin' t'compete wit' Houston, Fifth Ward, but it's nice."

She put her hand on my forearm. "You can take some clothes from the rack while I clean what you got."

"Thank you."

"I hope you like it while you here."

"I ain't too worried 'bout that, ma'am. I been a little sick an' I could use some sleep. But when I get better I'ma go get our car an' head back down t'Houston whether Mouse come back or not."

"Oh, he be back fo' then. Raymond ain't gonna miss no free ride."

"I hope not. But either way I'ma be gone by day after tomorrah at the latest."

"Uh-huh, yeah." A woman had come in the door and Miss Alexander went over to talk with her. As she left she said to Dom, "Show Easy this room in the back, honey."

"Yes, ma'am," the hunchback said.

Dom showed me to a little shack behind the store. It was put together pretty well and there was no need for heat. It had a spring bed against the wall and a crate table in the middle of the floor. There was a big tin pitcher full of water in the corner and sheets and towels neatly folded on the bed. There was a stack of old newspapers next to the door.

"I'ma leave you now, Easy. Momma want me t'come out to her place an' see her guests, an' Raymond might come by."

"You tell Mouse t'get his butt down here fo' I leave him."

"He be here soon, Easy. But you know he gotta finish up business wit' Reese first."

I wondered how much Dom knew about the crazy violence Mouse had in his heart for Daddy Reese.

"Can you read them papers, Dom?"

"Oh, yeah, I already read mosta them. Not all of it, but what I could. Them is Sweet William's papers."

"Who?"

"Sweet William. That's Miss Alexander's entertainment. He's a barber down in Jenkins but on the weekends he come up here t'play guitar an' sing."

"He reads?"

"Oh, yeah. William read the whole paper."

"Must be a lot in that."

"Uh-huh, Easy. Things you couldn't even believe if you ain't read 'em yourself. It use t'be that William read t'us an' I always say, 'No!' like I didn't believe what he said. I said, 'No!' an' that was it. But since I can read I know that a colored man runned a race in Europe an' beat all the rest of the runners of the world. Yeah, an' he was from America just like us. Uh-huh. You know, Bunny Drinkwater say that the best thing we can do is run, but that's just jealousy talkin'. Yeah. Readin' is sumpin'."

I wanted to ask him more but I was tired and a little shy of how ignorant I was. Being a young man I felt I should be able to do anything better than a hunchback, and the fact that I couldn't rubbed me wrong.

After Dom left I lay down on the bed and thought about things again. It was the first chance I'd had to collect myself in a few days and I wanted to get my head straight.

But no matter what I tried to think of, my mind went back to those dogs. I could see them jerk around as the bullets tore through their skinny bodies. Just a quick jerk and they hit the ground, dead. I had seen death before and not long after that I was in the World War where death came by the thousands and the tens of thousands; but I never felt so close to death as when I saw those dogs die. Just a twitch in the air and then they fell to earth, one by one, heavier than life can ever be.

I'd close my eyes but then I'd start awake thinking about what must've crossed before their dog eyes as they died; I was so upset that I couldn't sleep. I was afraid to sleep; afraid because I had seen death in a way where it was real for me and I worried that I'd never wake up. I wanted my father again; wanted him for the thousandth time since we ran out of that slaughterhouse and he ran out of my life forever. I wanted him to come back and protect me from death.

That's when I decided to learn how to read and write.

I looked at those papers and thought that if I could read what was in them I wouldn't have to think about those dogs; I thought that if I could read I wouldn't have to hang around people like Mouse to tell me stories, I could just read stories myself. And if I didn't like the stories I read then I could just change them the way Dom did with the Bible.

That was a big moment for me. And I'd say that the whole trip was worth it just for that, but I can't say that because I lived to tell about it and not everybody else did.

Just thinking about reading calmed me down enough to get

to sleep. I rested for a long time and then I found myself awake: I was lying back on the bed, staring out of the window, thinking how pretty the moon was. A man was sitting on the crate with a tin guitar in his lap, pulling on the frets and plucking odd notes. When he noticed my eyes he lit a match and set its flame to a candle at his feet.

"Well . . . you back wit' the livin', eh?"

He was a well-dressed, dark-skinned man. He was wearing a tapered white suit, like the deacons wear in church on Easter, and a black shirt with pearl buttons that were open down to the middle of his chest. His hair was long and processed straight back. His face was so clean and shiny that I remembered thinking that he must've shaved three times before he oiled his skin.

"They say you come out here wit' Mouse?"

"You call 'im that too?"

"Shee . . . I'm the one named him." Sweet William ran his red tongue along black lips. "You could say that I was a buildin' block that help t'make Mouse who he is."

"Might not be too much t'be proud'a," I said.

William leaned back and gave me a leery stare. "I thought you an' him was friends?"

"We are friends, yeah, but I been th'ough some things out here in the country, man . . . I wanna go back t'Houston."

Instead of talking he started playing a slow blues tune. I've always loved blues music; when you hear it there's something that happens in your body. Your heart and stomach and liver start to move to the music.

"What kinda things?" he asked, still playing.

"Things."

"Like what?"

He kept on playing.

"Man, I don't even know who you is. What you gonna be askin' me all this?"

"My name is William. I play music here on Friday an' Saturday. An' I wanna hear 'bout Mouse; I ain't seen him in, oh, 'bout four years. That's all, I don't mean nuthin'."

All this time and he was still playing his guitar.

I shook my head and said, "It's just that I ain't been in the country for a while an' it kinda gits t'me. An' Mouse don't know no normal peoples. He know witches an' hunchbacks an' old white ladies an' everything."

William's teeth were pure white.

"Yeah, that Mouse don't be foolin'. But you know folks is diff'rent from country than they is in the city." He was rocking back and forth to the rhythm. "In the city they all wear the same clothes and they get t'be like each other 'cause they live so close together. It's like trees; when they real close they all grow straight up to get they li'l bit'a sun. But out here you got room t'spread out. They ain't no two trees in a field look the same way. Maybe one is in the wind an' it grow on a slant or another one be next to a hill so one side is kinda shriveled from the afternoon shade." Then he began to hum a tune in a strained high voice that sent shivers down my backbone.

After a while he started talking again. "It's like my music; I ain't so good at it. Once Blind Lemon Jefferson played here; it was more'n fifteen years ago but I remember how good he played like it was last week. An' you know if ole Lemon lived 'round here I wouldn't never even look at a guitar. Why would I bother when I could hear him?

"But I can play out here an' be who I wanna be 'cause it's only me who does it. Uh-huh, uh," and he started his wordless song again. I could see where Mouse learned a lot from William. He was a smooth character from his slicked-back hair to his way of talking in song.

When he stopped again he asked me to come listen down in the store. "It ain't Houston but we get pretty wild on a Friday night. Uh-huh."

THEY HAD CLEARED OUT the tables from the center of the store and a dozen or more people were there drinking and talking. The cardplayers had moved their table into a corner. William went to his chair and started playing as soon as we walked in. Miss Alexander came over to give me a tumblerful of moonshine.

"You feelin' better, honey?" she asked.

I lied and said I was.

"How you like it out here so far?"

"It's pretty nice, ma'am. I'm not used to all this fresh air though."

She knew that I meant more than I was saying. She laughed and took me by the arm and introduced me to various folks.

". . . this is Nathaniel Peters," she said when we came up to a stout farmer with hamlike hands. "Our best farmer and minister. This here is Easy, Reverend."

"Please t'meetcha, son. I hope we see y'all on Sunday."

"If I'm still here, sir."

"Well . . . you know the Lord wants to see ya."

"Then I want you to meet a girlfriend'a mine, Theresa."

Miss Alexander turned and waved to a woman across the room. "Com'on over, honey, an' meet Easy."

"You from Houston, huh?" the skinny black girl said. She was missing one of her front teeth. "My cou'in Charlene live down there, on Avenue B."

"What's her last name?" I asked.

"Walker."

"Yeah, I think I know her. She like to dance?"

"That's Charlene," she laughed. "She love t'dance."

We lied like that and drank and danced to William's songs for the rest of the night. She told me all about her dreams and her plans and her family but I forgot everything she said; I was just being friendly. The only thing I remembered was that she told me how to get out to her house—which wasn't too very far away.

I don't remember passing out.

I woke up in the bed out back, alone and hungover.

CHAPTER

9

B Y THE TIME I HAD THE HEART to get out of bed it was noon. Miss Alexander was sitting at the counter in the back and the cardplayers were still at their table in the corner; Sweet William had joined them. He waved at me and I smiled, or at least I tried to.

"How you sleep, Easy?" he asked.

"Like a corpse," I groaned. "Woke up like one too. But when I looked in the closet I saw some clothes there . . . I din't mean t'kick you outta yo' room."

"They's lotsa beds in Pariah." He winked at me and for a second I felt like I was talking to Mouse.

I could see that Miss Alexander was waiting for me at her counter. I felt like a whole flock of wayward sheep; like I needed a herder to set me straight.

"You don't look so good, Easy," Miss Alexander said.

She was wearing a red dress that was so bright I had to look away.

"No, I just look bad right when I wake up," I said. I was sick but, like a fool, I didn't want to tell her because I was afraid that she'd keep me from leaving. "I be ready t'leave tomorrah mornin'."

"Ain't you gonna go t'church wit' us tomorrah?"

"I gotta be gittin' back."

"Even a sinner got a little time fo'the Lord, Easy."

"Well, maybe. . . . What time is the service?"

"Reverend's a farmer too, so he start early; us'ally 'bout eight." Then she smiled. "Theresa wasn't too happy 'bout you last night."

I felt my face flush.

"I think she likes you," Miss Alexander went on. "An' there you was laid out just like a pile'a dead wood."

She laughed and I did too.

"Why'ont you go over wit' the men an' I get you some food."

I SAT IN A CHAIR against the wall and listened to the men talk while they played. Miss Alexander brought me a plate of dirty rice and greens but I didn't have any stomach for it. I put the plate on the floor and a dog climbed out from under the table and wolfed it down. It looked like one of Reese's dogs; hungry, near death.

The men talked about everything: gardens and women and white people. It felt good to listen to them laugh and trade lies. It's good to be a man with no worries, among friends. I remember every story they told but, for the most part, they didn't have anything to do with me.

One of the men was called Buck. He was older, maybe sixty, and he had a high strained laugh.

"Hit me!" he said to William, then he flung down three cards. He was a sly cardplayer. You could tell he was tricky because every time he'd take some cards he'd try to keep the others' attention distracted by bringing up some shocking news.

"Reese Corn is dyin'," Buck said as he shuffled his cards.

I don't know how she could tell from across the room but Miss Alexander strolled over as soon as they started to talk about Reese.

"What?" That was a young man, tall and skinny, name of Murphy. I never did get his last name.

"It's true." Buck was studying his new cards. "My boy's girl was down there yestiday an' she said he looked bad." He looked up from his cards and smiled. "I raise ya five," and he pushed a nickel to the pot.

"What you talkin' 'bout, Buck?" Miss Alexander said.

"That's what Yolanda said." He hunched his shoulders.

"What's Yolanda doin' out to there anyway?"

"She do piecework. Ole Reese ain't bought a new shirt in thirty years but he cain't sew fo'shit neither. So Yolanda go out there every two months or so an' patch him up."

"I see ya," Murphy said.

"I'll take that an' I go up five." William threw two buffalo heads into the game.

"But the weird thing is his do'," Buck said, and then waited for one of the men to ask. No one took the bait, because they knew he was just trying to break their concentration.

But Miss Alexander didn't care about the game.

"What about his door?" she asked.

"It was painted black; jet black with cloves of garlic hangin' from it."

"Yeah?" Miss Alexander opened her eyes wide. "Maybe my sister come back t'haunt his evil soul."

"I meet ya, William, what you got?" Buck nodded. "I don't know what's happenin' wit'im, ma'am, but sumpin' got him scared; scared to death, almost."

Miss Alexander shook her wide mane. "Evil calls on itself."

"Amen," William said. "Pair'a red queens."

I could still see that doll hanging from the tree.

Later on in the game Murphy told William that he had been down to Jenkins the week before.

"Oh yeah?" William grinned. "You down at the saloon when Big Jim got there?"

"Mmmm-hm, you better believe it! He come in wit' that badge stuck in his hat an' that nightstick in his hand an' yell, 'You fellahs better duck,' an' he pult out that long-snout pistol he got." Murphy laughed. "Man, we was kissin' the boards like it was true love."

They all laughed. Jim was the colored deputy for the county. He was tough and mean and it seemed that he was pretty well liked in the district.

The gambling and talk went on that way. I leaned against the wall and faded in and out of sleep until a long time later.

Clifton came through the door in the late afternoon.

He looked worse than I felt. His clothes were soiled and so wrinkled that it was clear that he had been sleeping outside. His jaw was set so that he looked like he couldn't ever talk again. When I called to him he jumped and his hands started shaking. Then he turned, headed for the door. He would have run out if two men hadn't been walking in right then. He turned back to the room, then around to the door, but the men, just two old sharecroppers, were looking at him and he backed away. I got to him before he could run.

"What's wrong, Clifton? Someone after you?"

"Shut up!"

The look he gave me was the look of a hunted man; I'd seen it in my own father's face, and I respected it even in a fool like Clifton. I told him that I had a room in back and he was happy to go there. I sent him on, then I went over to Miss Alexander. She had watched the whole scene very closely.

"What's wrong wit' yo' friend, Easy?" she asked.

"I don't know yet but I'm fixin' t'find out when I get back there." Then I hesitated for a minute. "You been pretty good t'me, ma'am, but I have to tell ya that I ain't got no money right now, t'pay ya. I mean Mouse 'posed t'give me a little change but . . ."

"Don't you worry, Easy. Raymond sent a few dollars over wit' Dom the day 'fore you got here. I thought you knew."

"Uh-uh."

"Yeah! You want sumpin' fo' your friend?"

"Maybe some food and a little whiskey."

"Sure thing."

She went out to the kitchen and came back with a trayful of food and a half-full whiskey bottle. There was only one glass.

"Glass is fo' yo' friend, Easy. I don't think you need any more."

Clifton was standing in the corner of the room with his fists at his side, clenched just as tight as his mouth. He looked past me to see if anyone else was coming.

"Take it easy, Cliff."

When I handed him the tray he hunkered down on that crate, eating like a hungry animal.

He started in with the chicken and didn't even stop when he licked the plate clean. He took the chicken bones, cracked them open with his teeth, and sucked the marrow out from every one.

I went over to the bed to wait for him to finish; when I lay back I felt all the strength go out of me.

"What's your problem, Clifton?" I asked when he was through.

"What you mean?"

"Com'on, man, you know what I mean. What you doin' here shakin' like that and so hungry you eatin' bones?"

Clifton downed a whole glass of whiskey and doubled up trying to keep it down. I was sure he was going to vomit but he just put his hands on his knees and made snorting noises until he could straighten out.

"Yo' friend come out to the witch's house night before last."

"Yeah?"

"Uh-huh, an' he said that the word come down to a deputy out here called Jim, an' Jim is on my trail."

"He said that?"

"Then he say that I gots to run 'cause Jim is a quarter injun an' he always find what he looks fo'. He say I'm a sittin' duck out at the witch house so I better run."

"What Jo say?"

"Witch don't say nuthin'. She just ask yo' friend if it's true an' he say yeah." Clifton took another big drink and went through the same pain.

After he was sitting up again I asked, "Where's Ernestine?"

"He say that I cain't run wit' no girl so I should go alone. But I tole him that I ain't gonna listen t'that shit an' Ernestine comin' 'long wit' me!" Clifton yelled the last words and I could imagine Mouse smiling right then; it gave me goose-flesh. "But Ernestine tole me t'go. She said she don't wanna run from the law an' she said that I gotta take this on myself." Clifton wept and took another drink. "When I seen she ain't gonna come I said I be back but she said don't even bother wit' that."

He put his head to his knees and cried.

I was too weak to comfort him but I knew what was right. I knew that I should tell him everything I knew about Mouse; what a rotten man he was and how he messed with other people's lives. Even if Clifton didn't believe me I should have told him and then my conscience would've been clean. I should have taken that boy in the car and gone back home to Houston, but I was sick and tired. Even when he told me Mouse's plan I stayed quiet.

"Yo' friend tole me t'meet him t'night. He showed me a place in the woods where I could sleep an' then he said I should meet him t'night an' he gotta plan fo' me t'get away. I axed why he doin' all that for me an' he said he doin' it fo' Ernestine so the law don't get on her. So what can I do?"

I wake up nights remembering Clifton sitting there with his hands stretched out. I had the answers but I didn't give them to him because Mouse was my friend and you don't cross your friends.

Or maybe I just didn't care. Maybe that's what was wrong with us back then. Life was so hard that we were too tired from just living to lend a hand.

Clifton left after a while and I didn't even think about going with him. He knew that Mouse was up to no good but he needed someone else to say it so that he could change his mind.

He'd have been lucky if it was Big Jim on his trail.

THE SECOND-NIGHT drunk never feels as good as the first. I finished the whiskey and lay in a funk all night. I didn't sleep at all. I just had visions of people coming in and out of my room; some of them I knew and some I didn't.

My daddy came in and sat on the bed. He looked at me with sad eyes and I felt I had done something wrong. I asked why he never came back and he said that he died; that he wanted to come back but death was too much and he finally gave out.

Mouse came in with a young woman. He was talking to me but feeling on her at the same time. I asked him to stop but he said, "You know you like t'watch, Ease." And then he pulled out his thing, it was so big that the girl got scared but Mouse sweet-talked her and she said okay . . .

Then the door opened and Domaque came in. He stood next to the bed and said, "You up, Easy?"

"Do I look like I'm up?"

"Well . . . you lyin' down but yo' eyes is open. . . ."

I just waited for him to disappear like the rest of my dreams but then he said, "I wanted t'talk wit' someone, Easy. An' you Raymond's friend too. . . ." He went on, "I met that girl an' she real pretty, an' she be out to Momma's house."

"At Jo's?"

"Uh-huh. She called Ernestine an' I like her an' she said

she come out an' look at my house if Momma wanted her to."

"Yeah?"

"Uh-huh, Easy. She kinda pretty an' she wanna stay out to there wit' Momma. . . ."

When I saw the sky lightening into dawn the dreams went away. I knew that I had fever but it didn't matter because I was sure now that I had to go home. I was going to go to church with Miss Alexander and then I was going to find the road to Rags Pond. And when I got back to Houston I was going to learn how to read and write. That was all I knew; in that I guess I was lucky.

10

EASY! EASY! Time fo' church, hon!"

It was Miss Alexander calling from the door. I guess she didn't want to come into a man's room uninvited.

"All right," I called back. "I be up in minute." But I was asleep before my mouth closed.

In my sleep I saw my parents sitting at breakfast. My father was reading a paper even though he couldn't read. My mother was making griddle cakes, singing . . .

"Easy!" Miss Alexander was shaking my shoulder and calling in my ear. "We gotta go, honey! Jo gonna be there."

I remember sitting on the side of the bed with my head between my knees. I had fever and cramps and a pain in my head but I thought it would pass in a day; it's an amazing thing that young men get any older at all.

I'd slept in my clothes, which was lucky because I don't think I had the fingers to do buttons and zippers that morning.

Miss Alexander was wearing a plain white dress with a lace green hat and William wore a brown suit with black lines crisscrossing it. Momma Jo was with them. Domaque and Ernestine were behind her. Dom had on the same overalls he wore when I first met him and Ernestine still had on the blue dress with the red-brown cows printed on it. She'd washed that dress though and she had a necklace of tiny red flowers, the kind of flowers that grew at Domaque's house.

"Hi, Easy," Jo said in a soft voice. "You look a little tired, honey."

"Hi, Easy," Dom yelled. "This here is Ernestine."

"Easy," she said simply.

I looked down at her feet; they were still bare.

We all walked down to the building with the white crosses on the doors and went in. A woman sat at the front playing an upright piano. It was a lively tune but I couldn't put a name to it. Theresa was there in a nice violet-and-white dress; she came over and sat next to me. I recognized almost everybody from the dance at Miss Alexander's but I didn't remember any names so I just nodded when people said hello.

The room was almost full, about sixty souls there. A big woman and a shrimpy little man went up to the piano and started singing hymns. There was a hymnal underneath each chair and, one by one, people lifted them and started to sing along. I didn't because I have a bad voice and I just didn't feel up to it.

When I heard the door open in the middle of "Sweet Baby Jesus," I turned around to see who it was.

The chill I felt when I saw Daddy Reese was the cold that a corpse might feel.

He wasn't the same Reese that I had seen a few days before. That Reese was a powerful man, that Reese had muscle like black iron and a thick mane of nappy black hair. But the Reese who walked through that door on Sunday was an old man. His arms and chest sagged down like flab but he wasn't fat; he must've dropped ten pounds in those few days, I'd never seen a man lose weight so fast. His hair was sprinkled with white, not gray. He was stooped, just a little, and when he walked he had a slight limp.

Some men believe in evil. They've seen so much of it in the world and in themselves that it becomes a part of what they know as truth. And when you believe in it the way Daddy Reese must have, you open yourself up to people preying on that fear. The strength of hatred turns to weakness.

But with all that Reese was bowed—he wasn't broken. He was wearing a black suit, the old kind that my grandfather wore with five buttons on the jacket. He had a starched, high-collar white shirt and a hat kind of like a bowler.

When he saw me I thought he was going to come in my direction but just then Jo turned to see what I was looking at and that changed Reese's mind. He took a chair in the back.

Just about then the minister entered the room. Reverend Peters was a fat man with a wide mouth and a black suit; he strode down the middle aisle shaking hands and saying good morning to the people he passed. He was bristling with energy, the kind of man that pious women have sinful dreams about. The kind of man who feels so confident that other men don't like him too well.

"Mornin', brothers and sisters!" he shouted.

"Mornin', Reverend," said an old woman in a raspberry dress. She was sitting right up front.

"Yes, it is a good morning. Every one of God's mornings is a good one."

"Mmmmm-hm! That's a truf," the old woman said.

"And the only thing that's a bad mornin' is a mornin' that you wake up an' you don't find Jesus in your heart."

"Yes, Lord!" That was Miss Alexander.

"Oh, yeah! When you wake up and Jesus ain't wichya, then it truly is a bad day. Not only for you but for every one of us in the congregation!"

"Amen," a few voices said.

"Because Jesus loves ya! He loves ya and he wants you to do right. An' what is right? To have Jesus in your heart. That's all. Because if you got Jesus with ya you ain't never gonna do bad. Jesus won't let ya do bad if you let him in. He won't let you go astray. No he won't. The Lord is gonna stick by you just as long as you stick by him. He's gonna be a extra pair of eyes to see wrong . . ."

"Amen, brother, show me them eyes," the shrimpy man in the baggy pants said from the piano bench.

"I don't need to show you, Brother Decker. I don't need to show ya because the Lord will show you. He will show you out from temptation and you won't even feel bad because the love of the Lord is greater than money! It's greater than love of a woman or a man! It's greater than freedom!"

I could feel the congregation tense up at those last words.

"Yes, chirren, the love of the Lord is greater than any- thing you can have or desire. The love of the Lord is greater than anything." He stopped and ran his eyes across the congregation. "Anything that you can have or desire. Anything. If you see a new dress, sister, and you think that that dress is gonna make you as beautiful as Sheba, as beautiful as Cleopatra . . ." He stopped, looking around again, and then smiled a knowing smile. "But we all know that beauty passes, don't we?"

He opened his eyes wide, and a few laughs broke in the audience.

"You look in the mirror from one day to the next and you'll see what I mean." I glanced back at Reese.

The minister went on, "You young ones might not know it today, but don't worry, the Lord is gonna forgive ya. You give him a chance, a half a chance, just a glimmer, a bare sliver of a chance, and the Lord is gonna forgive ya. He will. I know it because he has saved me."

We were with him then, every soul in that church. And God was with us.

"I was a sinner. Oh yes, Lord, I was a big sinner. I lied and cheated and you know the Lord don't hold with no liar. I hated it but I couldn't help myself because if the Lord ain't wichya then you know that the devil is.

"If the Lord ain't wichya, you know the devil is.

"And the devil was with me and I did his handiwork. You do it too. Oh yes you do! Don't sit back there and tell me that the Lord don't slip away from you sometimes when you see another woman wearin' that pretty dress an' you cain't afford it. Don't tell me that 'cause that's a lie and lyin' is sin. Men and women is born to sin and the only way out is lettin' Jesus in your heart. You cain't help it, no you cain't. You men see a pretty girl an' you know what you feelin' is wrong but you cain't help it, you cain't. You not gonna do it by yo'self! You need the Lord to help you do right."

He paused and took a glass of water from the piano. Somehow he made drinking a part of the sermon. You could tell that his sermon had just come to him as if God had flown down into him as he took the podium. No one was talking, no one was looking around, no one shifted in their chair. God was in the room with us in the shape of a fat minister about the color of coffee with three spoons of cream stirred in.

Perspiration had broken out over the minister's forehead. He took a fine white handkerchief from his pocket and ran it across his brow, then wiped his hands. By the time he was finished with his hands his head was beaded up again.

"I'm sorry, brothers and sisters," he said with his head bowed. "I have another sermon to give and you know I don't believe in a long sermon but today something got in me. That happens sometimes. When you let the Lord in there's no tellin' what might happen. The Lord might pick you up and throw you across the world. You could be a young girl on the farm until the Lord picks you up and makes you a general at the head of a great army. Yes he can. . . . He might, he might." Reverend Peters got quiet then and it seemed like he'd lost his place. Sweat was running off his head but he didn't bother with it.

After a long moment he said, "You all know about Job. How he was a rich man and a family man, a man who had the respect of not only his fellow man but the love and the respect of God."

The words left such a silence in the room that I had to stifle an urge to shout.

"Yes." The minister was calm now. "God loved him but he needed Job to prove that he deserved that love. Oh yeah, because you got to prove yourself to the Lord. He's not gonna open up his great kingdom of heaven if you're not worthy. And how is he to know if you're worthy unless he tests you?

"And the Lord took away Job's thousands of sheep and took away his thousands of camel. The Lord brought disease, death, and division on Job's family. And when the Lord was through, Job was a terrible sight to behold. He'd lost his wife, his chirren, his money, his health, Job had even lost his self-respect. He tore at his breast and wished that he was never born! His friends and people betrayed him and God turned a deaf ear." When the minister looked out you could see tears rolling with the sweat down his face. "And Job doubted. Who wouldn't? Even if all you had was one dress and a tin pan—if someone took that and left you with nothin' you'd be tempted to despair. And we know that it's the devil causes despair. Think of Job; he was a rich man! A respected man! You don't let that go without some tears and some bitterness. But when he realized that all he had taken for granted could be taken from him, Job was amazed. He wasn't angry at God. He was angry that he had loved God for the wrong reasons. Because even in poverty, even with nothing, Job realized he had God within him. There was love and grace inside. And Job was saved.

"You might think that this is a simple story. Something you learn in Sunday school; a Bible story for children to remember if hard times should strike. And that's what I thought about it too. But you know I was turnin' soil last Thursday, 'cause you know I'm just like the rest of ya: son of a sharecropper, salt of the earth. I was watchin' the soil turn up under the plow like water in the wake of a great boat, and I thought, 'This land belongs to God.' It's for sure it don't belong to me or any of you here this morning. We all know whose name it is on the deeds to all our places and even on this buildin' we prayin' in."

I remembered Miss Dixon's fears and I thought that maybe she was right.

"I remembered the poverty of my daddy's sharecroppin' days. And I thought about Job; how the very ground from under him fell away and all he had left was the deaf ear of God. I wondered, 'What did Job eat when he had lost everything?' And I knew even then that Job scratched in the ground and hunted in the wild and he lived off fish from the lakes. He created a life from God's greatest gifts: the mind and the heart and the land too.

"You might wonder why I tell you this. It's because I see a day coming when the Lord is gonna test us. He's gonna pull the land away from us and he's gonna strike down with his open hand and smash away this village. He's gonna take it all and the only thing you'll have left is your wits and the love of Jesus in your hearts. You'll have to make your way against a terrible storm. Your hearts will be full of tears but remember, it's God testin' you. He's lookin' to see that you love him as the spirit, not just for the fleshly desires he can satisfy. And he needs to know that you will survive to praise his name."

The minister let his head fall forward. The room had the silence of grace in it. Everybody, from Reese Corn to Sweet William to Miss Alexander, everybody felt a mighty presence. Not necessarily a presence of love or even salvation. But there was truth in the room; it was almost solid it was so real.

"The land don't belong to you. No it don't. Your houses and your clothes and your chirren too. None'a them belong to you."

A small boy was sitting on the other side of Theresa, his eyes filled with tears.

"It's all the love of Jesus, the love of God. If he wants it, then he'll take it, an' it's not fo' us to question his infinite will. This life is just a test for your love an' your faith.

"I feel love for my land and my labors. I feel rage when I am being mistreated and cheated. But all that takes a backseat to the love of God." Reverend Peters was crying but his face was full of light. "And when the time comes it will be his scriptures I look to for my answers."

He bowed his head again.

Somehow he must have signaled the pianist because she started playing softly. Brother Decker got in front of the podium and said, "Sunday school will begin at half past nine at Miss Trevor's house. There will be a meeting of the church council directly after this service. . . ."

WE WERE ALL QUIET in the balmy morning outside the chapel. I wondered at the sermon's meaning. I could see something in what Miss Dixon told me. But there were parts that I just didn't understand. Why did I have to live so close to disaster? Why would God want that?

It was a mystery but I didn't have time to think about it because that's when I felt a hand on my shoulder.

"Where Raymond?" Daddy Reese asked me.

The whites of his eyes had gone yellow, and the smell of his breath was like the stench of a corpse. I told him that I hadn't seen Mouse in a few days.

He grabbed my wrist and leaned against me; he hissed into my face, "You tell him that I don't care what happens. I see my soul in hell fo' I let up on a dime, you hear that?"

"I hear ya, Reese."

"Not one fuckin' dime!"

"I ain't seen'im, Reese, an' I don't know when I'm gonna."

Reese pulled on my arm with one hand and went for his pocket with the other. He was weak and sick but I wasn't too spry myself. I don't know if I had the strength to hold him from cutting my throat.

"Hi, Reese," Momma Jo said. "Been a long time since I seen you at church."

At the sound of her voice Reese let me go and fell back. "Get away from me, witch. Get away from me." And he turned, running from her.

"What he want, Easy?"

"I dunno, Jo. He want Mouse, not me."

When we all walked back to the store Jo said to me, "I'm havin' supper wit' Domaque and Ernestine, Easy, why'ont you come on out?"

"I'm sick, Jo," I said to her feet. "I gotta get some rest."

She put her hand on my throat again.

"You is hot," she said.

11

WHEN I GOT TO THE ROOM a calm had set in on me. I was wondering if the minister was right. Was everything I experienced the whim of God or his test to see if I was worthy? I laid down on the bed and let the strength flow from my arms and legs; and in my weakness I gave up my responsibilities.

I thought about how Mouse was like Job's devil; how he had called Daddy Reese the devil. I didn't even care about the dogs.

When I opened my eyes Mouse was sitting on the crate facing me.

"How you feel, Ease?"

"Li'l sick I guess, but I'ma leave soon as I can walk down t'the car."

"Well, by then everything should be done." There was a serious tone in his voice, not the brash way he usually sounded.

"What you tryin' t'do, Raymond? What's all this mess wit' Clifton an' Ernestine an' Reese?"

"It's more than that. I got wheels turnin' all over. Wheels inside 'a wheels, like a great big ole clock."

I didn't have the strength to even ask him anything but he started talking again.

"Yo' daddy run out on you when you was a boy, right, Ease? I know that that prob'ly hurt you. You prob'ly want him back so bad. I know how it feel. I was hopin' fo'a daddy when I'as a chile. Momma loved me but you know kids ain't never satisfied so I wanted me a daddy too. I always be pesterin' her 'bout my real daddy, an' I knew I was hurtin' her. So she married Reese. She wouldn'ta done it if not for my pesterin'." Mouse's clear eyes had the light of honesty in them. "An' he kilt her. Abused her an' hurt her through me. Reese is a harsh man. A woods man. The kind of man that likes to hurt. She knew what he was but she did it for me."

Mouse clasped his hands between his knees. "So it's like I killed her by never bein' satisfied wit' what we had. 'Cause you know from the first day in that house me an' Reese was at it; an' me an' Navrochet, that's Reese's blood son—me an' Navrochet was at it too. They had my momma workin' and toilin' while they was just as mean as they could be. An' they come down on me too. I was young, Easy, an' I could take it. But they wore Momma out."

Sunlight came through the muslin curtains with a small breeze. I was breathing softly and watching the cloth wave; I had forgotten Mouse was there until he went on.

"I thought I had let it go. Before she died Momma borrowed some money from Sweet William an' sent me t'Houston when I was still just a kid. That was about the same time you come into town. I had me a new life an' I never even thought about Momma or Reese or Pariah at all. Cousin Pernell an' his wife Justine took good care'a me until I could see after myself. Momma axed Sweet William to drop by an' check in on me now and then." Mouse smiled. "I grew up like a weed an' all I cared about was my friends and a good time. But Etta changed that. It's not like she reminds me'a Momma or nuthin' like that; you know my momma was a slight girl with a little smile and soft ways. But it's what we did together kept remindin' me of the ole days 'fo' she married Reese.

"You know Etta always have breakfast waitin' fo'me in the mo'nin'. I got a hundred girls suck my dick all night long but who gonna worry 'bout how I be eatin' in the mo'nin'? An' when we talk she know how I feel. An' when I love her I always be thinkin' 'bout babies; I see her sucklin' my son. . . . An' then you know what I be thinkin'? I think about Reese. I think about how he hurt me an' how he kilt Momma an' I know he gotta pay fo'it. That's why I come out here; 'cause Momma wanna see me wit' a fine weddin'. If she was alive she'd get a church and all her friends and they'd cook fo'a week and she wouldn't let me lift a finger or spend a dime. An' since she cain't do it I'ma make sure that Reese do it fo'her."

I wanted to talk to him. I wanted to warn him about Reese and ask him just to come back home with me. But I couldn't bring myself to do it. I was sick but I don't think I was too sick to talk. I just felt helpless. What was I going to do? Raymond couldn't help what he was; Raymond couldn't stop himself. That's what I thought then; maybe it was true.

"But now, Easy, I'm scared," Mouse said. " 'Cause I know I got Reese by his nuts wit' that doll. He from voodoo country an' a curse gonna tear him up, I know that. But now I'm ascared he gonna die fo' I get what's mine. My li'l spies be tellin' me 'bout how Reese is sick. But I gotta have that man's money. He cain't die 'fore that."

Then he was still, sitting there wringing his hands. I didn't have anything to say or maybe it was all a dream. Because I had a terrible fever that night. There was nothing I could do to stop what was going to happen. And as much as I knew I didn't know everything, I'd like to think that if I knew what Mouse's plans were I'd've tried to stop him right then. But maybe what happened was ordained like that minister said. Maybe it really was out of my hands.

It wasn't until years later, after the war, that I understood about Mouse; long after I'd learned to read and write I came across the meaning of the word that described him: inspiration. Raymond wasn't smarter than the next man; he didn't do anything new in the world. But he created lead from gold. He created his revenge on Reese from his love of EttaMae or maybe he found that revenge in her love of him. He changed the world to fit his twisted feelings.

Raymond was an artist. He always said that a poor man has got to work with flesh and blood. "Po' man ain't got time t'be worryin' 'bout finery, Ease; po' man cain't even watch his own ass, 'cause you know if you so much as flinch down here that's all she wrote fo' you."

I KEPT FADING OUT and coming awake again to see Mouse sitting there, wringing his hands and thinking. Finally I opened my eyes and he was gone. That's when the fever set in and I was lost.

WE WERE RUNNING out of the slaughterhouse and everybody was yelling. One man grabbed my father but he sent that man to the floor. Another man came up and he went down too. I noticed then that the rest yelled but they kept their distance.

We ran out into the truck yard in front of the building and down an alley. My father had picked me up into his arms and he was running fast. You could see the fear in his face, and that fear is what I remembered most. A scared little colored man with a child in his arms; the world shaking up and down like it was about to break apart and we were panting like dogs on the run.

Only dogs are hunters and we were hunted.

We ran down to the stream, where we had been trawling for crayfish not three days before, and fell into a heap. My father was breathing so hard that his throat sang.

"You gotta run up home, Ezekiel," he said to me. "You gotta go up the back way an' get yo' momma an' them an' go down t'Momma Lindsay's. You hear me, Ezekiel?"

"Yes, Daddy."

"I love you, boy."

"Where you be?"

"I gotta run right now, son. I don't know where I end up but I tell ya when I get there."

"You gonna come get us?"

He said, "Take care'a yo'self, boy," then he kissed me on the lips and hurried me on my way. And then I was a man running down the path yelling for my mother but never getting there.

❋   ❋   ❋

THERE WAS SOMETHING tickling my stomach. I looked down and saw a white cloth taped to my belly; it was writhing against me. I reached out to pull it away but a big black hand grabbed my hand and tied it to the bedpost.

MY MOTHER AND I SAT in the parlor of Momma Lindsay's house. My mother was on a chair and I was sprawled out on the couch. I was thirsty and she had made lemonade. Everything was natural except that a line of black ants ran down from the arm of her chair, they seemed to be coming from her clothes, and I was a full-grown man—I knew that she had been dead for many years.

"Where's Daddy, Momma?" I asked.

"I don't know, honey," she said. She was smiling at me with so much love. . . .

"But I wanna know where he gone. He said he gonna come get us."

She just kept on smiling, nodding slightly. The ants had cut across her forehead and they made a sound like bees buzzing.

Out of the window there were clothes on the line. The wind was blowing hard and they flapped so violently that I was afraid they'd blow off completely.

Then I'd have no clothes to wear.

I was aware of being naked on the couch so I sat up and crossed my legs. I was hoping that Momma would leave so I could go save my clothes before they blew away. But she just kept smiling at me with the ants all over her and the buzzing coming louder and louder.

❋   ❋   ❋

I WAS RUNNING OUT into the bright and windy day; all my clothes had blown away. I ran full out in an open grassy field. The blades of grass beat against my bare ankles, pelicans and gulls glided far above.

"What you callin' fo', honey?" a voice asked.

"My daddy!" I yelled, not like a man at all.

"Where is he, Easy?"

"He's gone," I said and then the world started to cry. Everything was tears and crying. I was so thirsty that I started sticking my tongue out and praying for rain. But the rain didn't come.

"EASY, YOU CAIN'T be worried 'bout every little thing," Mouse was saying. We were in my house drinking beer from green quart bottles. " 'Cause a po' man ain't got that kinda lux'ry. Shit! If all you got is two po'k chops an' ten chirren what you gonna do?"

I waited for him to answer the question but he didn't. He just stood up and walked out of the house. He was laughing to himself. I could feel the sweat pouring down my face.

12

"Res' NOW, EASY," Jo said.

She was swaying in a homemade rocker at the foot of the bed; a giant mother in a child's small room. The chair and the floor creaked as she moved forward and back.

There was vapor rising from behind her. The room was hot. "Water," I croaked. I didn't even recognize my own voice.

When she rose I was filled with awe at the size and might of her. I remembered the armadillos and that severed head. It was nighttime again and felt like I was back in the bayou, out behind those stunted pears.

She lifted my head to pour water into my mouth from a liquor bottle. She'd tip a spoonful in and wait for me to swallow, then she'd pour another one. When the water hit my empty stomach I got small cramps that quivered down through the intestines. But I didn't complain—the water tasted too good for any complaints.

"You been real sick, baby. Ev'rybody been worried. Dom an' Mouse an' li'l ole Ernestine. You had us all goin'.'"

"How long?"

"It's just been twenty-four hours but it was close. If I had come in the next morning rather than right after Sunday school we'd be plannin' yo' funeral right now. It's been comin' on ya for a few days. Miss Alexander say you was drinkin' an' I was mad that she let you do it."

When she stroked my face I felt the rasp of my stubble against her hand.

I fell asleep with my head on her lap.

Later I woke up and she was still cradling me. I was so happy then.

"Thank you," I said.

She grinned at me. "Baby, you better rest some more. The fever gone but you still weak, it could come back, and it's always harder gettin' rid'a it the second time."

"What is it?"

"I seen it before. It's a kind of poison that gets in ya an' acks like grippe but it ain't. You gotta use some old-time medicine to get that. Lucky you got ole Momma Jo t'fix ya."

I pressed my head against her thigh and she smiled down on me like she had smiled down on Raymond when I first saw her in the woods.

When I woke again it was night. Jo was rocking and embroidering. I thought it was strange that a woman like her would take up needle and thread.

"Could I have some water please, Jo?" I said.

"How you doin', Easy?" She brought me the liquor bottle.

"Fine."

"You lookin' good. I guess we gonna have you a li'l while longer, huh?"

"I guess." I raised myself to be fed the water and then lay back. There was still vapor rising from behind the rocker. I must've been staring at it because Jo said, "Just some herbs in water on a oil burner. Keeps it warm inside and keeps yo' lungs clear so you don't get pneumonia. You feel like you can have some broth, baby?"

I wasn't hungry but I said yes, I needed some strength. I felt the life coming into me.

Not exactly the same life I'd almost left behind.

When Jo came back Miss Alexander stuck her head in the door and smiled. "Hi, Easy," she said. "Glad to see you feelin' better."

Jo had a steaming bowl of beef broth with a big shank bone in it. She propped me on her knee and fed me spoon by spoon.

"You seen Mouse?" I asked her.

"Oh yeah," she said reluctantly. "He been around. He tole me t'tell you that he'd be ready t'go when you feel better."

"Where is he?"

"No tellin' wit' Raymond but he prob'ly wit' some girl. I think he been hangin' 'round Miss Alexander's li'l friend— Theresa."

I felt a flash of jealousy but it went away as soon as it came.

"So he wanna go home, huh?" I let out a short laugh and it hurt me on my stomach. "I guess he finished up whatever crazy nonsense he had wit' Reese."

"I guess so," Jo said as she pushed the spoon into my mouth just a little too hard. "So I guess you be headin' back home when you get to your feet?"

"Uh-huh, that's right. You know Houston cain't get along wit'out me for more'n a few days."

"Yeah." She smiled with me and I was glad.

It seemed like the only thing I'd ever done was to sit alone with Jo in the night. And I was liking her pretty much then too. I was thinking about what Mouse had said about not turning up your nose at a woman like her.

"Easy?"

"Yeah, Jo?"

She let my head down on the pillow and went back to her chair. She sat down with a sigh and said, "I been thinkin' 'bout what happened out to the house, baby. You know, wit' us. And I feel kinda bad cause'a what you must be thinkin', so I just wanna tell ya 'bout how I feel."

She took a deep breath that brought me back to the night we were lovers.

"You could see that I ain't a normal woman. I got big bones and I'm taller than almost any man I ever seen. An' I ain't like big girls neither. Us'ally a big girl sag down an' be quiet hopin' that a man won't notice her size—but I cain't do that. I'm loud and rough and I'm pretty smart too. It's not that I'm vain, Easy, I'm just tellin' it like it is. I'm better than most men at bein' like a man. Domaque was the on'y man was my match." She had a lost look in her eye and I knew how she felt after all I had remembered about my father and losing him. "And he was too good to live. On'y reason I stay out to that house is because I'd be more alone wit' people. 'Cause if I come in on a situation an' I know what's right, then I'ma do what's right. And if a man, even a white man, stand up an' be stupid then I just set him straight. I mean women can be wrong too an' they can be just as dumb as any man. But a woman us'ally come around quicker than a man 'cause if you hurt a man's pride you might as well give up on him ever thinkin' right.

"Mens don't like a woman big as I am, not if they manlike too. They wanna feel they power but they don't want none'a yours. But I could see you wasn't like that." She gave me that shy smile. "They is somethin' diff'rent in you, Easy, somethin' soft. It's like you looked at me an' said, 'Okay, this here is one big woman; now let's get on wit' it.' An' you didn't worry 'bout it no more. You didn't look at me wit' them big eyes like you was scared or like I'm a animal you gotta train. I liked that.

"That's why I done that mess wit' Ernestine an' that sour boy she was wit'."

I thought about Domaque and Clifton then.

"What's she gonna do now that Clifton's gone?"

"She wanna learn some things I know an' . . ." She looked down and smiled. "She been goin' out to Dom's house t'pick flowers wit' him. I cain't hope she gonna be no more than friends wit' him but Dom sure could use the company."

"I like you, Jo." I held my hand out to her. She came over to hold it.

"That's all I wanted, baby. I know I shouldn'ta done what I did. I wanted you t'be my friend. I mean I cain't ask you to wanna be out here wit' me . . ." she said, but there was hope in her voice.

"I couldn't, Jo. I mean, I could love you but it would turn out bad." I wanted to say yes, to say that Mouse was right.

"I gotta stand up fo'myself, Jo, an' I just couldn't do that wit' you, out here." I should have just said that she was too much woman for me—that's what I felt. I lied about everything back then. There just wasn't any truth to be had.

We talked for a long time, about everything. She told me stories about her and how she kept things going out around Pariah. She delivered babies, made potions, and settled disputes. I told her about wanting to read and about women I'd known. We were fast friends, holding hands and talking the night away.

But whenever I'd mention Mouse she started talking about something else. She told no stories about him when he lived there and if I asked she'd just say, "Oh you know Raymond; he ain't nuthin' but bad news wit' a grin."

Finally I asked, "How come you won't talk about him?"

"I don't wanna be thinkin' 'bout Raymond now, Easy. I know he yo' frien' an' I ain't got nuthin' good t'say."

"But he brung that girl down."

"I'm thankful fo' Ernestine but Raymond din't make her. An' all his foolin' 'round ain't helpin' my boy."

"What he do?"

"I don't know nuthin' 'bout what Raymond be doin'."

"But I bet you could guess." I smiled at her but she didn't smile back.

"All I know is that I seen Raymond an' that Clifton headed out Blacksmith Row, out toward Reese Corn's place. They left when the sun was goin' down."

The tone in her voice spoke of violence. All the drowsy recuperation in my brain burned off like morning mist. Sweat formed on my forehead and hands. I gulped once because of the nausea that accompanied the decision I made.

My stomach rumbled.

"You hungry, huh, Easy?" Jo asked.

"Yeah, yeah. Hey, Jo, could you go'n get me sumpin' t'eat?"

"I got some bread an' fruit right here in my basket."

"Naw," I said. The sick frown on my face came naturally from the sour pitch in my gut. "Couldn't you go'n get me some hot soup or sumpin'?"

"It's late, Easy," she whispered, to show me that she was afraid of waking people up.

I stared at her while thinking about my own dangerous purposes. Maybe it was the fear showing through my eyes that moved Jo.

"Okay," she said. "I'll go see what I can find."

She kissed me. It was the natural brush of lips against skin. I imagined prehistoric wolves making the same gesture with their snouts before they howled as men, women, and children sat shivering in their caves.

I COUNTED TO TEN and pushed myself up out of the bed.
I fell to the floor before I could manage even one step. It
felt like I should have been able to walk but my legs just
wouldn't listen.

There, on my knees on the floor, I noticed the broad cloth
bandage held to my stomach by a thick gray goo slathered
around the edges. I leaned back against the bed and pulled
the cloth away.

The skin underneath was puckered and discolored. Under
the cloth was a stack of leaves and twigs; in the middle of that
nest was a dead toad.

The toad was plump and looked almost as if it were still
alive. When it fell away I saw that there was an open cut in the
shape of a cross, two inches either way, above my navel. The
toad's belly had an identical cut.

*   *   *

I CAME AROUND the side of Miss Alexander's place and turned left. When I got to the end of the street I turned right and walked until I came to a pecan tree. Two houses past that was a small cabin, a hut really.

My knock was answered almost immediately in spite of the late hour.

"Who is it?"

"It's Easy Rawlins, Theresa," I said through the rough-hewn plank door.

When she pushed the door open I was forced to take a step backward. She was wearing a burlap sack with holes cut for her head and arms. The candle she held showed me that the holes for her arms were a little too big, I could see her left breast sticking out of the side.

"What you want, Easy?"

"Raymond here?"

No words came to her.

"I asked you is Raymond here, Theresa."

She shook her head and it was my turn to keep quiet.

"He gone out to Reese," she said at last.

I was staring at her breast and thinking that Raymond would have called me a fool for worrying about things that were none of my business. Then Theresa pointed out the way to me when I told her that Raymond would be mad if she didn't.

I MADE IT OUT THE SLIM PASSAGE through the woods thinking about all the steps I'd taken to bring me to that path. It came to me that it all started when my father ran away from that butcher and out of my life. He never called for us. One day I came home from school and our neighbor was waiting there for me. When she told me that my mother had some kind of stroke I wasn't even surprised. I had expected her to leave too.

I've been counting my steps from that day to this one. From Louisiana to Texas; from childhood to being a man.

I wasn't quite yet a man as I walked down that country path. But I was headed for maturity. I had driven Mouse out there and anything he did was a reflection on me.

It was the noble thought of a fool.

DAWN WAS FILLING the woods with a cold glow when I heard the voices. One of them was Mouse, his hard-edged voice loud and threatening. I couldn't understand his words but at least I knew they were words, spoken to be understood.

The reply was a single note of rage.

I followed the murderous sound even though I knew I should have gone the way of my father.

I came to a stand of cherry trees on a small hill above Reese Corn's place. Clifton and Mouse were standing near a large woven bamboo basket. Mouse was holding his big .41 over his head while cocking his head to make sense out of the scream, which was coming from the basket.

Clifton was armed with a shotgun; he was holding it by the twin barrels.

"What's that you say, Reese?" Mouse shouted at the basket.

I could see the lid stuttering against the latches it had been secured with. I was close enough to hear the pounding blows. Reese must have done that with his head and shoulders and back.

It was a large basket but Reese would have had to squat down, hugging his knees and bowing his head, for them to have closed the lid.

"Let'im go, man!" Clifton shouted. "Let'im go!"

The next thing Clifton, or I, knew, Mouse had his pistol pointed at the boy's nose. Raymond said something but I couldn't make it out.

I took a step from the stand of trees. Clifton bowed his head. Reese Corn bellowed. The sun, which wasn't the least bit concerned with that drama, peeked down through the mist.

I took another step and stopped.

Mouse turned to the basket and shouted, mimicking Reese's hoarse rage. The basket shook from the internal blows.

I had taken three steps when Mouse started kicking the basket. I felt that if I walked slowly and calmly into that situation I could stop all the hostile activities. I honestly believed that I could calm Mouse down and bring Reese around to reason.

Maybe I could have done all that.

"Let'im alone!" Clifton shouted.

The boy thrust out his free hand and grabbed Raymond just when he was in the middle of a kick. The kick went wide, slamming against one of the bamboo latches that secured the lid.

Mouse hit the ground squeezing off a shot that hit the ground not two feet to my left.

The lid to the basket popped off and Daddy Reese Corn came out like a leaping jack-in-the-box. Blacker than Momma

Jo and naked, Reese went at the first target he saw—Clifton.

Clifton.

The only thought in my mind was to save that sour boy's life. I ran full out with my eyes wide and focused on the men.

Clifton took a step backward and raised the shotgun by the barrel, like a club. And then Reese was on him.

The gun seemed to leap into Reese's hand of its own accord. It twisted like a snake and Reese's hand was at the trigger.

I yelled.

Clifton did too. Then the blast hit him.

Mouse had made it to his feet but Reese was faster that day.

Reese turned toward his stepson before Clifton hit the ground. Mouse fired but Reese ducked low and rammed Raymond with his shoulder.

Mouse's second shot went somewhere in the trees.

There was no savoring the moment for Daddy Reese. Mouse was rolling away on the ground, toward his dropped pistol. Reese was drawing his bead.

Neither one of them heard me coming on.

I had no plan, or dexterity to execute a plan if I had one. I didn't grab Reese. I didn't even tackle him. I simply ran into him like a fool running into a brick wall.

I felt the recoil before hearing the shotgun blast.

The air went out of my lungs and the ground came up to meet my face.

"EASY," HE SAID SOFTLY. "Easy, wake up."

Mouse was squatting down next to me. Beyond him I could make out a black arm sprawled on the ground.

Mouse pulled me up by my shirt. When I was standing I looked down on Reese. A large part of his left temple was gone. The shotgun lay at his side.

Clifton hadn't died all at once. He'd been gut-shot. He'd ripped off his shirt and pulled down his pants to try and do something about the wound. He died with both hands trying to push the intestines back into his body.

Mouse's pistol lay near Clifton's shoulder.

"Come on, Easy. We got to get outta here."

I was light-headed, staggering behind Raymond. Many times I stopped because there was something I had to remember and I couldn't walk and remember at the same time. Whatever it was I needed to recall was like a reflection in water and every step I took sent ripples across the image. So I'd stop. But before the image came clear Mouse would shake me and say, "Come on, Easy, we ain't got time t'play."

I remember walking behind him, seeing that he still had that tan rucksack hanging from his shoulder. It looked like it was stuffed with clothes. No more Johnnie Walker.

MOUSE BROUGHT ME in the back way of his aunt's store. I went to my little room and stretched out on the thin mattress. I dreamed that I was a stone in a field lodged among different kinds of grasses. The growth of the grass made the scrunching sound that a finger makes when it's pressed across the tight skin of a drum. By midsummer the grass had grown over me and I was in the dark shade of towering blades of green.

14

REESE CORN WAS A SOLITARY MAN in his last years. He didn't come much to Ethiopia Baptist Church. And those of you who don't have faith," and Reverend Peters looked out over the congregation, "might say that he had lost the way of the Lord. But Brother Reese didn't lose his way. He knew death was comin' an' on his last Sunday in the world Reese came back to the Lord."

"Amen," Mouse said. He was standing next to the open coffin, his gloved hands folded before him. He wore a spotless black suit with a black tie and an ivory-white shirt. I never did know where he found that outfit.

"Yes, he came to the Lord at the last moment, but you know that's enough for Jesus." He surveyed us again. "All Jesus needs is for you to look his way an' he's gonna save your soul. That's why we're here; to be saved. All'a you here today are alive but you're gonna have to face it too. Yes you are.

Every one of you in this room is going to have his moment of reckoning and her moment of reckoning and in that moment you will have to take Jesus to your heart, or you will perish."

I thought of Reese's dogs and went cold somewhere; that one spot in my heart has never kindled again.

"I believe that in his final moments Reese Corn opened his heart and he was saved.

"You all knew Reese. Miss Alexander was his sister-in-law. Nine years ago we laid her loving sister to rest."

Miss Alexander sat next to me. Her eyes were dry and there was a slight smile on her face.

"You know when Reese's wife died . . ." Reverend Peters leaned his elbows upon the podium. "He was broken. You could see that he lost faith because he let his house fall into disrepair. He didn't have any kind words to say because he felt that the Lord had abandoned him. He stopped saying good morning and left the church. He lived a lonely mean life out there on his farm, and who knows? Maybe that loneliness called out to the poor boy who followed him there. Maybe it was the Lord in his infinite wisdom calling Reese Corn home."

Ernestine started crying, and Jo folded the girl under her arm.

"That boy was a messenger of the Lord, calling out. And once Reese came back to the Lord's house that messenger was sent to Reese. Because everything we do is governed by God. If you wake up in the morning and hear the whippoorwill or if you meet a young girl and fall in love, that's God workin' on ya. If you find yourself full of strength choppin' cotton on a beautiful Tuesday morning and you breathe in the sweet smell of earth, well you know the Lord is with you then." The minister held up his opened hands and stared into his palms, then he put them back down. "But when your babies get grippe and the life burns out of them before your eyes; when you tear at your clothes and beg God to take you instead; when you're left in the room with a dead child innocent as can be—the Lord is with you then too."

"Yes Lord!" the old woman, in the same raspberry dress, shouted.

"Yes the Lord is a hard master! Because you know you cain't raise a child right if you don't raise your hand." He paused. "And we are the Lord's chirren. Reese and that boy Clifton were the Lord's chirren. He's called them home. And in callin' them home he's taught us a lesson; a hard lesson. In despair comes ruin, in despair comes ruin. Reese tore down his house. Yes he did. He knocked the what-do-you-call-'em?" He looked around as if there were someone there to answer. "Yeah, he knocked down the beams, the main beam of his house, and the walls fell in. The walls fell in on Reese and he turned his back on the Lord. There's a lesson in that. I don't know what happened to that boy Clifton. I hear that he was a violent man, a man who lived by violence. It's said, I don't know if it's true, but it's said that he killed someone in Houston."

The minister looked up at the ceiling and shook his head as if he were arguing with the next words the Lord was putting into his mouth. Finally he returned his gaze to earth. "What is our lesson? That's what you wanna know. What is God trying to say to me here today? Well . . . no one can truly understand the mind of God because the mind of God is what we call infinite. That means he's everywhere. As far as you can go—God is there. He's at the bottom of the ocean and he's way out past the moon and stars. He's in this room right now, sittin' next to ya. Reese is with him now, and if Reese could pierce the veil, I think he'd say the lesson is the infinite forgiveness of the Lord. . . ."

The minister kept going in that vein but I was distracted by an amazing sight: There were tears streaming down Mouse's face. He was crying outright. You'd think that real love was pouring out of his heart onto the floor at his dead stepfather's feet. "What could it be?" I thought, but no answer came.

Miss Alexander leaned to my ear and whispered, "I want you t'com'on wit' me when it's over, Easy. I wanna make sure that bastard who kilt my sister is dead."

Those were the only words that crossed her lips about Reese. And it came to me that they were all happy to see him dead. The minister had remarked that it was "the Lord's infinite mind that called his stepson back," to be there when Reese died.

Reese was a hard man and an angry man. He had turned the whole world against him and no one cared to look beyond what seemed to be the story.

It was told that Reese was out at his house when a fugitive from Houston came upon him to steal his money. The fugitive, Clifton, had heard that Reese was rich from Raymond Alexander, who was coming to tell Reese about his coming marriage. Reese shot Clifton but Clifton managed to get his gun and shoot Reese before he died. Mouse came upon them when he'd come to tell Reese that he was returning to Houston.

There was no money found.

Big Jim, the colored deputy, was at the funeral, and I think he suspected that there was more to the story. But you don't go doing police work for a colored killing when you got an answer lying cold at the back of the barber's shop.

Jim warned Mouse that Navrochet wouldn't take it so easy. He said that Mouse's stepbrother would wonder at how Clifton got to Pariah. But Mouse just smiled and shook his head.

". . . The Lord is with you, brothers and sisters . . . keep him in your hearts. Because no matter how hard you hurt, he will comfort you as he did Brother Reese in his last moments. Amen."

"Amen," we all said.

"TIME T'GO, EASE," Mouse said. We were standing in Miss Alexander's general store. Everyone was there. There was homemade wine and cornbread and people from all over the county. Theresa was standing next to Mouse; she and Ernestine were the only ones who truly looked sad; they both lost men that day.

"Yeah, I'm ready," I said. I couldn't even look him in the eye.

"Easy." Her voice came from behind me.

"Yeah, Jo."

"I guess you ain't comin' back out here soon."

"I don't know, Jo. You never can tell what might happen."

"Well I think me an' Dom an' Ernestine might be comin' to the weddin'."

"You know I'll be there." I looked up into her flat, dark eyes. She put her hand to my throat again.

"Bye, Easy!" Domaque yelled. He and Ernestine were standing close together behind Jo.

"Bye, Dom. I'ma start my readin' soon as I get home."

Dom gave me a strong handshake and a crooked smile. He said, "Remember to make it in yo' own words, Easy. That's how ya do it."

The car had been moved to the edge of town by one of Mouse's friends. He'd gotten the key from my pocket when I was sick. Raymond hefted the stuffed rucksack on his shoulder.

"Weddin' gifts," he said.

I wondered if Theresa was coming to the wedding.

Just before we left for the car Miss Alexander took me by the arm to an empty spot on the wooden sidewalk.

"Easy, I'm glad you're feelin' better . . ."

"I been meanin' t'thank you . . ."

She waved her hand for me to keep quiet. "I feel bad that you ain't seen us in a good light, Ezekiel. You know we was all glad to meet you and have you with us. It's always nice to meet one'a Raymond's boyfriends, he got a real knack at gettin' friends."

We shook hands and then she kissed me on the cheek.

Sweet William and Mouse were standing next to the car when I got there. They were the same height and looked so much alike that you would have had to be blind not to see the relationship.

I don't think Mouse ever suspected that William was his father. Some men are just lucky.

"Well, Easy, I guess you gonna get back to the city to rest from the country, huh?" William smiled.

"Yeah, you country people is too wild for me."

He shook my hand. The rest of them came up and waved to us; Theresa ran to the window and kissed Mouse on the lips.

"She sure have grown," Mouse said to himself as we took off.

IT HAD BEEN GRAY all morning but the drizzle didn't start until we left Pariah. It wasn't a rain that cleaned the leaves of dust but a mist that changed the dust to caked mud on everything. The whole world turned filthy and streaked.

Mouse said some things to me but I ignored him for the most part. There was a weight on me. It seemed like the air was too heavy and that the trees along the road were so loose that any minute they'd crash down on us. My fingers felt thick and numb.

Mouse was smoking store-bought cigarettes and whistling; you'd've thought the sun was shining on him.

When we got to the main road the bugs came out. We smashed them by the dozens on the windshield. They exploded into blossoms of blood and body parts, then they slipped away into the thin film of drizzle. Every time we hit one I thought of Clifton, with his dour expression, sitting in the backseat; I thought of Reese on his knees in front of his broken house.

There were dead animals in the road too. Armadillos, porcupines and even a couple of dogs. Cars ran them over in the night and kept on going.

Their bodies were torn open and they still seemed to be bleeding because the rain had kept the blood fresh. Flesh burst from the fur like cotton from a ripped sofa.

"Here ya go, Ease, maybe this brighten up yo' face." Mouse put a fat envelope, folded from a sheet of newspaper, on the dashboard in front of me.

"What's that?"

"I might not be able t'read like ole Dom but I can count like anything," he said.

Another time that might have gotten a rise out of me but those days were over.

"Yeah," Mouse said. "I cain't read but I can count to three hundred in my sleep."

I didn't say a word. I wouldn't even look at the envelope.

"What's wrong wichyou, man?" he asked me.

"Ain't nuthin wrong."

"Then why you cain't even talk?"

"Ain't got nuthin t'say, that's all."

"Yeah. I know." He stared at me for a moment, then went on, "Easy, I want you t'take that money. It's yours an' it would be a insult t'me if you leave it lyin' there fo'Otum t'take."

I said, "Where you get that money?"

"Fount it."

"Fount it where?"

"Out t'Reese's place. I mean he got a will say ev'rything go to Navrochet. But you know he owed me sumpin' so I just look at it like this here money I got is mines."

"How much was it?"

He pointed to the envelope. "That there's just a piece of it."

I was quiet again.

"You wanna know what happened, huh?" He was grinning at me.

"I don't wanna know nuthin'."

"Yeah you do. You think I did sumpin' wrong, don't you? You think I murdered Reese, don't you?"

Mouse sat back and put his foot on the dash. He was getting ready to tell me another story, but I had lost my love of his tales.

"Ya see, Ease, it started wit' Clifton. I knew he could he'p convince Reese about gettin' up offa that money an' I also knew that Ernestine was young enough and wild enough an' she like Jo enough that she might give Dom a li'l pussy. You know Dom could use some'a that. So I went an' tole Big Jim 'bout what I knew 'bout Clifton."

"You tole the law?"

"Yeah, I can't be lyin' 'round Jo 'cause she so good she even got me. Anyway, Clifton did beat that boy so it ain't like I was lyin' t'Jim. Only I didn't tell Jim where Clifton was. Ya see, I'as givin' him a chance."

"Uh-huh!"

"I had Clifton buried out in the woods at night while I was layin' up wit' Theresa. I tole him that I was watchin' for Jim. Clifton was so scared that he couldn't even sleep. He'da done anything I said. So I warned 'im that Big Jim was gonna get'im sooner or later unless he got far away, an' then I tole him 'bout Reese's money.

"Ya see, I figgered we'd rob Reese; it was my due anyway. An' Clifton went along wit' it after some convincin'. I give Clifton a shotgun I borrowed from Sweet William. I tole Reese Clifton was a killer an' we was gonna have it. He was a mess, Easy. He smelled from garlic; I guess he thought that would save him from voodoo. It was pitiful." There was glee in Mouse's voice. "But I was gonna have that money. We put'im in that bamboo basket an' told'im we was gonna shoot'im 'less he climb outta there an' show us to the money."

Mouse was savoring every moment of the torture. He really believed that he hadn't done anything wrong.

"But then that fool Clifton had to grab me an' th'ow off my kick. If you'd hadn'ta run Reese down I'd be dead now. Shit. I'm lucky my gun landed near Clifton, 'cause you know Reese woulda beat me t'death with that shotgun."

"An' then you fount the money?" I asked.

"Yeah." Mouse was staring out over the panorama of his brilliant future. He saw black-and-white dice through glasses of amber whiskey. He saw EttaMae in cashmere and silk. Somewhere there were children calling out, "Daddy." And all the while Reese lay in the ground, turning to sludge.

"If you fount that money when he was dead, then why couldn't you have fount it when he was packed in that box?"

Mouse laid those cold eyes on me.

"Yeah," he said. "You right."

"And I don't believe it, Raymond."

"You'ont believe what?"

"I don't believe that Clifton shot Reese. That boy had his hands full tryin' t'hold his guts in."

It was like I had forgotten who I was, and where I was, and who I was with. Maybe it was because I had a full stomach and I sat behind the wheel of a nice car. Maybe it was all that money up on the dashboard.

For a moment there I thought that the truth was more important than the need to survive.

Mouse winced and nodded. I realized that I had caught him in a lie.

"You right," he said again.

I turned away from his cold stare only to see the red blood of a fat bug smear across the windshield.

"An' that's why I need ya t'take this here money, Ease." He pointed at the envelope again. "Because you the on'y one got my confidence. You the on'y one know why I come down here an' you the on'y one know what happened. If you don't take that money then I know you against me." He looked at me with a plain face.

But this time that face wasn't hiding laughter. His voice was the whisper of death, the slither of a snake over the nape of my neck.

Death had always been a part of my life. He lived in my neighborhood, in my apartment building, right next door to me. But I'd never worried about him coming knocking. I was innocent and I knew that I would live forever.

But at that moment I realized that the wrong words would cut my life down to seconds or, at the most, just a few days. And I also knew that whatever I said would be my first words as a man in this world.

I reached out for the bundle and said, "Thanks, Ray."

Mouse laughed and slapped my knee.

I had survived again. I had risked my life to save Clifton only to fail. But I had survived that failure. I was following in my father's fleet footsteps: standing up when I couldn't take any more and then running to fight another day.

Mouse started telling me how hungry Theresa was for love. I didn't care.

When we saw Houston in the distance Mouse said, "You know, Easy, when I was standin' there listenin' t'Peters preach, somethin' touched me, I don't know if it was God or the devil or what, but it felt like all the pain and fear I ever known was gone. I been scared'a Reese day and night for my whole life and now he's dead." A smile of pure joy spread across his face; tears sprouted from his eyes. "An' I'ma be married and I'ma be happy fo' the rest'a my years."

B ACK IN THOSE DAYS rent was two dollars a week and you could eat your fill on a quarter a day. I had three hundred dollars; I could've lived for more than a year on that.

But I wasn't careful. I bought a quart bottle of bourbon every other day and sat in that room, stinking and drinking. Most of the time I was too drunk to worry about it. But late at night the demons would come at me.

I was a part of the murder of a man's father. Me, Ezekiel Rawlins, the man who worried after his own father for years. It's not that I cared for Reese but murder is a sin that burns your soul.

And to help a man murder his father . . .

People came to my door but I didn't answer it. They'd knock and call my name but I'd lie in the bed and bite my pillow. I'd shut my eyes tight against the sound and finally they'd leave.

Mouse would come to the door and call me. He'd rattle the doorknob and bang away. He talked to me as if he believed I was in, but I didn't answer him. Our business was over with. There was nothing left to say.

Even today, six years later, I feel guilt and fear. The same fear I had when I thought my father knew everything that I did wrong; every thought that I thought wrong.

How could I have known? I asked myself.

How can anyone hold me responsible for the death of that man and that boy?

But then I'd think of standing there with Miss Alexander looking down on that wasted frame of flesh on brittle bones. A man who I helped to torment; a man whose murder goes unavenged.

I was unworthy. In my misery I told myself that that was why my own father never came back for me.

My mother was a churchgoer but I never had much use for it. Just as soon as I was old enough to hold back I fought with her on Sunday mornings so I could go out exploring the country and see my friends.

On Sundays my friend Holly, short for Hollister, and I would go to Tyler's place out John Street because on Sunday mornings Lucy Jennings, the whore, would be there entertaining all of the husbands who got out of going to church. We hid in the bushes outside of her window and watched. I remember holding my breath when Robert Green would stand in front of her with his thing standing straight out; it was so big that we couldn't believe it, Lucy told him that it was the most beautiful one she had ever seen. . . . When I got home I felt guilty but I couldn't tell my mother about it, it was so dirty and depraved.

I couldn't tell anyone about Reese and Clifton either.

For the first time I thought about God. I wondered if he'd forgive me like Reverend Peters said. But I didn't see how he could. I wasn't going to the law, I wasn't going to give myself up. I loved freedom and life and the only thing that would come from confessing was prison and death.

I took Mouse's money. It's true I was afraid not to take it but I didn't throw it away. I could have found a worthy cause and given up my loot for that but I didn't, and I wasn't intending to do it.

All I could do was to lay up in my room and drink.

If things had continued like that I would have died there in Houston all those years ago; I'd've never learned to live with my guilt and remorse.

But then something happened.

Every time Mouse had come to the door he talked, as if I were in, about the wedding and how they wanted me for best man. I couldn't talk to him. I sure couldn't stand in a room full of people knowing what I knew.

Then one day a knock came at the door. It came again and a voice said, "Easy?"

It was EttaMae.

"Easy, I know you're in there," she said. "And I'm gonna wait here at the door until you open up and let me in."

That's all she said. I put my ear against the door and after a while I heard a rustle, so I tiptoed to my bed and bit the pillow. After what seemed like a long while I snuck back to the door and listened; and just when I was sure she'd gone I heard her sigh.

Etta was going to wait until I was ready to open up.

I moved quietly to the window but when I looked outside the sun was so bright and there were people in the street that knew my name; I went back to the room. As quiet as I could I went around picking up the clothes and trash from the floor; I pushed it all under the bed and into the closet. Then I went to the door—she was still there.

I got the pan of water from the closet and tried to wash away the smell of two weeks without bathing. And then I changed my clothes. All I had decent was an old pair of cutoff shorts and a flannel shirt. I rolled up the sleeves because it was so hot.

When I opened the door she was standing there; I was planning to act surprised like I had just gotten up but I knew when our eyes met that there was no sense in lying.

"Easy." She smiled. Her dark brown eyes and deep brown skin were so beautiful. It seemed like years since I had seen her but she was still the same. Big and beautiful and so tender that I knew I would have crossed Mouse to have her for mine.

"Can I come in, honey?"

I stepped back and she walked by me. She was wearing jasmine, I remember. I never thought much about perfume before but right then jasmine became my favorite.

"Ev'rybody been lookin fo' you, Easy. How come you been hidin'?"

"Kinda sick, Etta."

"Raymond said that you come down wit' sumpin' in Pariah," she said. "He said that's why you took so long out there."

We sat down together on the bed. She put her arm around me and pressed my head down on her shoulder.

"You gonna get well to be our best man?"

"I dunno, Etta, I been real sick."

She put her hand on my forehead. "You don't feel hot."

"But I'm sick."

With her arm still around me she turned to my face and said, "I know sumpin' happened 'tween you an' Raymond out there, honey. I don't know what it was an' I don't wanna know. But I do know that you two is friends an' that Raymond will be sick if you don't stand up for him. Outside'a me you the on'y close friend he got."

I was looking down into her lap. She raised my face with her fingers and said, "Easy, you know we care for you. I been worried ever since I heard how you been actin'. No matter what's wrong, baby, you gonna have to stand up to it."

"What if I cain't stand no more?"

"Then you have to die, Easy. 'Cause when po' people like us stop movin' fo'ward then we die. You know we cain't hardly afford no vacation."

It was my first good laugh in weeks.

It must've been a strange laugh though, because Etta said, "Come here, honey," and when she held me the laugh almost turned to tears.

I went through a whole war and I never cried and I never got sick. I saw my best friends die right there next to me with nothing more than a sigh but I felt less then than I felt in Etta's embrace. I served under Patton where we froze and fought and then marched until we couldn't march anymore; and when we couldn't march we fought again; but I never even sniffled out there in those foreign lands. I was never wounded.

I did things far more terrible than Mouse could ever imagine but it never bothered me.

When she told me that I would die if I didn't stand I knew it was true. I understood that I was alone and there was no one there to help me. Reese was dead, Clifton was dead, but I was alive. There was nothing more I could do; I was just a man.

I got Etta a drink. I sat across from her on the chair and asked her all about the wedding. She told me that it was going to be on Saturday, four days away, and that it was going to be held around the gazebo behind Victory Church. She was near tears herself, she was so happy about it.

I told her to tell Mouse not to worry. I'd be there with a tux and a smile. But I said that I couldn't come to rehearsal because I was still sick and there was a lot to prepare. We hugged and laughed for the next hour. I felt closer to her as a friend than a lover.

After she left I went down to the Jewish tailor on Claxton to rent a tuxedo. Then I went to the train station to buy my ticket.

Late that night I went to the bathroom down the hall and bathed and shaved and got myself back together.

I slept for twenty hours after that.

When I woke up it was early evening. The sun was just down and people were in the street. Some were sitting out in front of their houses and others were wandering around; going to work or looking for a good time. I broke out some cheese and chocolate and brought a chair to the window. Watching them soothed me. People living their lives. I believed that they all had secrets like mine but they kept on moving.

At about midnight a fight broke out between two men who

had been drinking together on a stoop across the street. They'd been throwing dice for an hour before one of them called the other one a liar.

I watched them beat each other. I saw the short one pull out a knife. The fat one grabbed at his chest and staggered down the street, one hand clutching the wall. A woman was screaming and people ran around like ants. I just watched it; I knew that my day would come and I was in no rush to get there.

THAT WAS THE LONGEST MONTH of my life. Every minute stands out like an hour; every hour stands out like a day. I met the strangest people and went to places that I could never have imagined. I lost what a religious man would call his soul.

Pariah is gone.

Miss Dixon died a month after Mouse was married and her relatives came down from Chicago to split up the land. They leveled Pariah and moved all of the people out of the area. They charged back rent on the land, so everyone ran away; they didn't have any money. Momma Jo and Domaque and Ernestine disappeared too. They didn't come to Mouse's wedding. I think that he didn't want stories about Reese's death to be around when he had so much cash.

On that Saturday every soul that I knew in Houston was at the biggest wedding Victory Church ever had. There must have been two hundred people there. Flattop and Lips brought their band to play at the reception. Little Red was there, and Jellyhead, with his greased-back and conked hairdo. All of Mouse's old girlfriends came; Etta's admirers were there with them.

It was something else.

Etta and Raymond walked up to the gazebo. The minister stood there waiting. A breeze was blowing and the pastel silk flags that hung from the roof of the gazebo waved like angels calling out the great day. There were children who could barely hold in their excitement. The women were in fine dress; all of them in tears. I wondered if they cried because Mouse was going off the market or because they were so happy or because they knew how hard Etta's life would be with a man like that. The bachelors were standing around snickering and wondering what being married meant—not in much of a hurry to test it out themselves.

The minister asked his questions and the wind blew harder. I stood there next to Raymond. He was sharp as a tack and so cool that you could almost see the mist rising from him. His eye was certain. Etta was beautiful at his side.

"I do," Mouse said.

And when the question was asked of Etta she hesitated for just a second, less than that. And I remembered those boys Mouse had told me about; the ones that killed rats on the docks down in Galveston. I wondered how well Etta would stand up to Mouse's harsh life but I was still happy for her. She was taking her chance and that's all we can do in this life.

The party moved to the social club across the street. Flattop's trio played music of the modern age: jazz. And we danced and drank hard until the milkman came to join us. Some people left the party to go to morning service in the church.

Etta kissed every man twice and Mouse got a chair and just watched her. He was so calm and so happy that it was hard for me to remember him desperate or mean.

"Hey, Easy," Otum Chenier said to me when the party had just begun.

"Hiya, Otum."

"Mouse say you two took my car down to Pariah fo'a week."

"Uh . . ." I didn't know what to say.

"He give me the money." Otum opened up into a smile. "I guess you did right. I mean, I could use that twenty-five."

He laughed and I did too.

"How's yo' momma, Otum?"

"You know that's what get me. Lucinda got that call 'bout Momma but when I got down there they said they didn't call. I had me a good time though. You know what they got up here cain't compare to the food they got down there." He patted his solid potbelly.

I said, "Drink up, Otum, whiskey gonna run all night."

"Yessir!"

The party was right. People came from all over Fifth Ward and beyond. There were churchgoers and gangsters, day laborers and cotton choppers from the farm. There were Mouse's best friends and people we never knew who just heard about the party somewhere and came by to help us celebrate.

". . . an' help themselves," Mouse said with a smile.

Everyone said that it was the best party that they had ever been to; it was even more than that for me.

I was feeling romantic that night. It wasn't that I was looking for a woman; I had lost my wild passion for young girls
after that night with Jo. Jo showed me something about love.
She showed me that I didn't know what it was. . . . But I wasn't
feeling romantic toward a woman; I felt that way about my
life—the life I had lived in Fifth Ward for years.

All of my friends, and people who could have been my
friends, were dancing and drinking. Some of them were
around Mouse, listening to his wild stories. It was so beautiful
but it was my last night there. It was Mouse's wedding party
and it was my good-bye.

I couldn't live with those people anymore. They were living
on the edge of despair; like those two friends fighting on my
street. I had the image that we were all, all of us in Houston
and Pariah, living between Miss Dixon and Mouse. It was a
deadly line we had to walk and the only thing that kept us
going was some kind of faith. Either you believed in God or
family or love. I didn't believe in any of those things anymore.
Maybe I never had.

So I had a ticket for Dallas, Texas, in my breast pocket and
a hundred dollars in my pocket. I was as happy as I could be at
that party because I felt safe. I felt safer with that ticket in my
pocket than I would have felt with a gun.

They couldn't hurt me anymore. Mouse couldn't come
banging on my door in the middle of the night. Married
women and old witches couldn't seduce me on dirt floors.

I needed a place where life was a little easier and where
nobody knew me. I knew that if I could be alone I could make
it. All the people around me dancing, having a good time;
they were just holding me back, wanting me to be the same

old poor Easy—not a nickel in my pocket or a dream in my head.

I didn't have a thing, just like everybody around me; all the money I had was in my pocket and all the clothes I had were on my back. That's how life was back then. You couldn't hold me responsible for anything because I didn't have anything. And, realizing that, it was time for me to go.

"Hey, Easy." Mouse strolled up, pleased as he could be.

"Sumpin' else, man."

"Ain't it." He flashed a smile. "I'm really happy you stood by me, Ease."

"I wou'n'ta missed it, Raymond."

We shook hands.

"I'ma take me a little trip after the weddin'," I said. "Gonna see what it's like back east."

"Uh-huh." He watched me closely. "You think they got sumpin' out there you want?"

"We'll see." I was looking him directly in the eye.

"You take care, Easy," he said. Those were the last words we spoke.

TEXAS BY TRAIN IS A REAL DESERT. They have miles of flat gray stone and tumbleweeds blowing and plenty of nothing.

I watched the desolate earth through my reflection in the window with a deep feeling inside me. I was the only one who cared about my leaving. No mother or father to wonder where I was. I could be dead; Mouse could have shot me for refusing his gift and who would have known? He would come back to Houston and Etta would ask him, "Where's Easy, baby?" and

he would answer, "Easy say he gone up to California, babe."
And that would be it. I'd just be a corpse moldering under
some bridge or an ornament on Jo's mantel.

Poor men like me are no more than a pair of hands to work,
if there's work to be had.

THE TRAIN WAS LOADED with people. All those Texans
headed north. The only car with room to stretch out in was the
colored car in back. There was just a few of us.

Sitting across from me in the almost empty car was an
elderly couple from Galveston. He had a bent back from
working around the docks for so many years and she had the
peaceful face of a woman who is most at home in church.

They were quiet and well-dressed, though I suspected that
the clothes they wore were their only good clothes. He was
very black and thin. She was the color of light sand. Her head
and shoulders were small but the rest of her body blossomed
out into a bulb of a body.

I didn't talk to them much at first; I was too busy feeling
the sweet pain of leaving. But I looked past them at the door
to the car once when a porter came in to sit down and smoke a
cigarette. She caught my eye then.

Her name was Clementine and her husband's was
Theodore. Russell was their last name.

"We goin' t'live with our son in California," she said, and he
smiled.

"What's his name?"

"John Alvin is what we called him. He has three brothers
and a sister, but she died last spring."

"I'm sorry to hear it."

"It was terrible. Her husband passed just three months before, it was that influenza. Cut young people down like wheat."

Mr. Russell said, "It was a shame but John Alvin took his niece and nephew an' now he sent us a ticket." He smiled, showing me at least three missing teeth. "Yeah, he's some boy."

"Sounds like it," I said. "What is it he works at?"

"They let him be a machinist at the Arthur airplane factory out there. They need smart boys in them places. You should meet John Alvin, I bet he could help you find some work too."

California was a little too far away for me then. At least I had heard of people going to Dallas. No. California would have to wait.

I saw three people die the first week I was in Dallas; two car accidents and a heart attack. I didn't get a good job but I got gardening work. I learned how to read just about well enough that when Uncle Sam called on me he put me in a tent with a typewriter, with a rifle under my desk.

But through all of that I dreamt about Reese and Clifton almost every week. They were always covered with blood, gasping as if they were just about to die. But they didn't die. They grabbed at Mouse's cuffs while he was sitting in a big chair counting out my three hundred dollars.

"I don't know what you worried 'bout, Ease," he said as he rubbed a blister of blood with the corner of a five-dollar bill. "You ain't done nuthin', man."

NOW I'VE BEEN THROUGH a world war and I'm on my way back home. They've given us three weeks R&R in Paris. I've got a room at the Hotel Lutétia on the Boulevard Raspail. This hotel was recently vacated by the Gestapo and now houses our military elite. I got a room here because I saved a white major's ass in the front lines and so he thinks I'm a hero.

I got tired of all the white soldiers calling me a coward for working behind the lines. So when the call came up for any soldier, black or white, to volunteer for Patton's push I raised my hand. Maybe I thought I could make up for my failure in Pariah.

But being a white man's hero doesn't make any difference to me. Maybe that's why I've spent the last two weeks remembering what happened in Pariah, and looking at the Eiffel Tower, rather than thinking about this white man's war.

Maybe, if I have a son one day, and he asks me about the war, I'll tell him about the time I had in Pariah. I'll tell him that that was my real war.

WHEN THEY ASKED ME where home was I said Houston. It wasn't until that night, hours after I was asleep, that I realized I had bought a ticket back to Etta and Raymond and everything I had left behind.

But it didn't bother me. There were gangs of white American soldiers roaming the streets, killing solitary black enlisted men. There were gangs of black soldiers getting their revenge.

All over Paris there were thieves, escaping Nazis, and loaded guns in hungry men's hands. I had a transport ship to survive and America yet to see again. Every step could mean death to a black man like me.

Why worry about the destination when the road is full of vipers? Mouse is probably dead by now anyway. How could a man so violent and reckless survive? And if he has endured, then married life has changed him. Maybe he's fat now, working as a cook in some hotel.

There's no way for me to tell the future from this room in Paris. All I can do is follow my footsteps, not at all like my father, and go back home.